Kailin Gow

Blood Ring

PULSE Vampire Series Book 9

kailin gow

Blood Ring (Pulse #9)

Blood Ring (PULSE Vampire Series Book 9)

Kailin Gow

DEDICATION

This book series is dedicated to all the nameless volunteer blood donors, my doctor, and nurses at Las Colinas Medical Center in Texas who helped me pull through when I had suffered extreme blood loss, blacked out, and nearly hit my head on the floor. Your team gave me bags of blood for transfusion, which helped restore me to a level of safety.

My body craved the blood to keep alive, yet the thought of having to receive the blood from others because my own body couldn't generate it fast enough, made me empathize with vampires like Jaegar and Stuart.

When faced with death by blood loss, you realize how precious that blood in your veins and that beat in your heart are. Thank you blood donors around the world for providing this pulse for me and everyone who may at one point or another require your gift.

Sincerely,

Kailin

Prologue

She was close to the Crystal River, now, with the ring in hand, the ring that would allow her to cross up....the river was shining before her.

"Hold it." A cocky male voice. The voice of a mere youth.

"What do you want, minion?" she snarled. "How were you able to follow me to this place?'

"It's Jaegar to you, Your Highness." The Pursuer. He was the one chasing her through the air just now. His words were dripping with sarcasm. "Maybe this will explain it." He flashed her a ring of his own... "Looks like diamonds are a boy's best friend, huh? Especially magic diamonds like these. Made with crystals from the Crystal River, right? I did my research."

"How did you get that?"

"Let's just say I'm good with my hands?" Jaegar said. "And that's nothing compared to what these hands are going to do to you. You hurt and almost killed everyone I love. Now, it's time for my revenge. So you're not going to cross, my dear. Not if I can help it. It's time for you to pay for what you've done."

A growl almost inhuman, came from a space on the other side of the icy river. No mortal eyes can see beyond the river to see the enormous brown wolf, one that had shifted, crouching there, ready to pounce. A werewolf. A guardian. Werewolves and vampires had always been at odds with each other. No, even at war with each other. This one was also fey. One of the wolf fey from Feyland. And he was determined to stop her from passing through from the mortal world to the land of the fey.

"Who are you to stop me, wolf!" Nereti sneered.

"The Prince," the wolf shifted into a very handsome tall and muscular young man with chestnut hair and hazel eyes. He appeared to be in his early 20s, as a human. Nereti had seen and ruled many mortal and vampire men before, but this wolf fey was quite extraordinary. His broad shoulders and confident stature reminded her of Octavius, yet his kind eyes brought Stuart Greystone to mind. As he stepped forward past the border of the Ring of Ice protecting the portal between Feyland and the Land Beyond the Crystal River, his shape became more solid and his voice boomed loud enough to announce his entrance. "I am Logan, the Wolf Fey Prince, and guardian of these borders."

Jaegar's blue eyes nearly bulged out of his sockets. "Damn, what do they feed you over there, genetically-enhanced dog food?"

Logan took one look at Jaegar and smirked. "More like ground minotaurs and an occasional vampire or dark fey, as we call you guys, over there."

"I thought werewolves were fictional," Jaegar said, scratching his head. "Of all the years I've been a vampire I've never encountered one...until now."

6

Kailin Gow

Logan laughed. "My ancestors did an awesome job spinning that tale and making us into some kind of legend out here. The stories began long ago when one of our wolf fey began transforming into a wolf and then was seen walking upright like a man, while still in transformation." Logan peered down at Jaegar. "I travel back and forth all the time between Feyland and The Crystal Realms, but I haven't seen you before."

"That's because I've never been this close to that portal there, what is it? A wall of ice?"

Nereti was peering at the wall, where icicles formed a circular ring. "I see the Winter Lands there. Feyland, the origin of magic, the birthplace of mine."

Logan stepped forward to block Nereti from moving closer to the ring of ice. He raised his sword that glinted wickedly from the small ray of light from the moon. "You, Dark Fey, and enemy to humans and fey alike, will have to go through me to get back to Feyland. I know your plans...you are seeking ultimate power of both Feyland and the Crystal Realms. I can't let you claim that."

Jaegar stepped forth too, facing Nereti and crossing his arms over his chest. "Seems like I'm in agreement with the Wolf. I can't let you do that, too, Witchy Poo. Trying to take over the human world is bad enough, but now that place of his, what do you call it? It appears a bit frosty there..."

"Feyland," Logan said.

"Feyland, thank you," Jaegar said to Logan before turning to face Neriti. "You do just a little too much of taking. I know because I have always taken what I wanted, too, but no, not like you. You make me look like a generous donor. All that greed you have...well, it's time to start giving back."

Logan stared hard at Neriti as though he was able to see right through her. "No, it can't be," he said. "I think I remembered being told about you

8

from fey history...the first fey to be cast out of Feyland...Pixie King Delano's first wife who committed the most heinous crime that threatens the boundaries between all that is supernatural and human. With all the murders that you committed of fey and humans alike in order to sustain your beauty and power, you created the curse which now this young vampire bears for eternity. Not only were you a Pixie Queen who put the idea into Delano's head to start a war between the Summer and Winter Kingdom, but you opened the portals between Feyland and the Dark Worlds to let the witches into Feyland where they practice their sith ways of deceiving the public with their lies, getting families and authorities to trust them and then slaughtering, sacrificing fey children and virgins to you. So evil are you and your witches that you sacrificed your own children, offering their souls up to demons in order for you to keep your wealth and position."

"Holy Mother..." Jaegar let out a big breath. "I had no idea you were that evil...I mean, you take the cake in the holy grail of evil, Neriti."

Blood Ring (Pulse #9)

Logan looked over at Jaegar. "So you see, there is no way in hell this woman will ever get back into Feyland or any of the Frost Worlds, or as you would like to call it, the supernatural world...if I can help it."

Nereti stood up straighter, her eyes glittering with mirth and arrogance. "Too late, Wolf Prince. The thing about being a fey and a vampire? We can glamour and compel. We are faster than fey. And as a vampire, we can transport ourselves a great distance in a flash."

Logan looked over at the shattered wall of ice and saw a figure, dressed like Nereti running across the frozen waters of the Crystal River. He glanced back at Nereti, and in a flash, she was gone.

He looked accusingly at Jaegar, who looked just as dumbfounded as he did.

"I saw as much as you did," Jaegar said. "And believe me, that came out of nowhere." He groaned as Logan shook his head and gave a great big wolf howl, alerting the Wolf Fey from the other side of the wall in Feyland about Neriti and got ready to jump through the wall to give chase to the running figure.

10

Jaegar groaned. "I am getting too old for this, chasing rogue vampires around. Now Neriti's escaped...how am I supposed to tell Kal and the gang back home I've let the biggest evil that ever walked the Earth out of my sight?"

Logan grabbed Jaegar's wrist and pulled him with him almost through the portal when Jaegar tried to fight him off. "Let me go now, Wolf!" Jaegar said.

"No, I have to keep an eye on you, too," Logan said. "Plus you know something about her that we can find useful."

"I say, let me go!" Jaegar struggled against the strong grip the Wolf Prince had on him. "If you don't," Jaegar said after a few more attempts to free himself, "then this invisible being holding only my other wrist will get through and..."

Logan sliced through the air between Jaegar's other wrist and what appeared to be nothing, and heard a woman's cry in pain. "Beast!" she spat, before materializing into Neriti. "Looks like I have to fight against you two before I can get anywhere..."

Jaegar and Logan looked at each other and turned their heads back to nod at Neriti. "Yup!"

Chapter 1

Neriti prepared for battle. She had fought long and hard for countless centuries ever since she was banished from Feyland, for this moment to re-enter her homeland. These two – the Wolf Prince and the vampire knight from the Consortium would be nothing compared to the vampires and vampire hunters she had faced in the Land Beyond the Crystal River.

She laughed. "Well then, come at me with all you've got. I wouldn't want to waste my breath on anyone unworthy of my challenge. Unlike your beloved Carrier, Kalina, my blood contains no impurities. I am the one true Queen of the Vampires, and soon of all. Every human should bow down to me." She looked at Logan. "Every fey will taste my bitter revenge for casting me out of Feyland and into the dark abyss, the Gorge, the belly of despair and destruction..."

"You got your just punishment, Dark Fey,"

Blood Ring (Pulse #9)

Logan growled. "It is against our laws that a fey enter into the Land Beyond the Crystal River to kidnap and commit murder of humans. You were guilty of trespassing, murder of 50 counts, and numerous atrocities. It is by sheer mercy of the old Queens and Kings of Ancient Feyland that you were allowed to live, that you were merely banished. By you showing up here, with your declaration, I, Logan, Wolf Fey, Prince of the Feyland Forest, will try my best to defeat you."

Neriti couldn't help admire the young Prince's bravery. He would die a swift death for it she noted. As for that vampire who once thought he was General Octavius' equal in claiming Kalina's heart, let's see how he would fare when she use her other powers on him. Even the great General Octavius fell and became her servant. With this cocky run-of-mouth one who acted more like an adolescent hothead, she would conquer him in less than two moves.

She looked into his brilliant blue eyes, which even for a vampire, was exquisite. "Anything to say before I turn you into dust?"

Jaegar lunged at her, "Why I..." But Logan held him back by holding out his hand.

"We strike together, not apart."

Jaegar looked at this young man who was in his early 20s. Wise strategy for someone so young and calm.

"Trust me," Logan said. "I've fought enough fey to know."

"She's vampire."

"Vampires are Dark Fey. They are part of the Dark Hordes of Feyland. They have been banished."

"I see," Jaegar said. "Fey as in fae, as in fairies, as in the wee little folks," Jaegar made a gesture like he was doing a jig.

"Oh brother," Logan said. "Lucky I sense there is some good in you or else you'll be the one I'll be doing this to..."

Logan lifted his imperial golden sword, forged by the Swordmasters of the Summer Kingdom, and sliced the air in direct path to Neriti. A golden flash struck Neriti, and she stumbled back, her face wincing in pain, while her black and red silk robe tied at the waist by an obie red sash, tore in long thin rips along the sleeves and leg area. Neriti had blocked the full force of the sword's blow but her elegant robes were no match.

"Trying to undress me?" Neriti asked in a seductive tone. "There are better and more enjoyable ways to do that, Wolf," she grinned.

Logan looked away. He was not going to succumb to this Dark Fey's charms. No doubt she would have some fey magic left, despite being banished...which meant, she was remarkably dangerous especially in the land of the mortals.

"You may look like Kal, but you can't tempt me. What I've learned from being nearly a thousand year old vampire with a young man's face and body is that beauty comes from within. You should know that, older-than-dirt Queen."

"Ouch," Neriti said, narrowing her eyes. "Harsh words for the one who was rejected. You, minion, are an outcast like I. She chose to save Octavius, and left you fighting off my vampires, while she went to save her love. She didn't care if you perished. Now who is the harsher of us? Your heart is dying with jealousy and bitterness for always being

16

in the shadows of your General, doing his bidding, giving up the woman you love for him. Don't you feel hate? Don't you feel rage?"

Jaegar was about to give some smart alecky remark, but looked down at the ground and at the ring on his finger. He was going to give Kalina this ring...after the battle with Neriti was over. It wasn't a diamond ring, but it was a crystal one, made from the magic of the fey.

"That ring on your finger, Minion," Neriti said, watching Jaegar's emotions play all over his face. She laughed. "You all thought it was real diamonds. You are like those worthless small-minded greedy humans you protect. No, that ring contains the magic of immortality. Not the kind we vampires know. Ours is just an existence. Immortality known to the fey is true power, true life... If you only knew how valuable those rings are..."

Logan gulped. "Like Prince Kian's snowflake pendant...the one he gave to Queen Breena."

"Who? What?" Jaegar shook his head. "What are you talking about, Wolfman?"

"Kian is the King of the Winter Court in

Feyland. Breena, ah, Breena is..." Logan's eyes became wistful, and it was clear what Logan felt for Breena was what Jaegar felt for Kalina.

"I don't care who she is," Neriti said. "They will all bow to me soon in time."

"Breena bows to no one!" Logan roared. "She didn't come all the way from Oregon to unite all the kingdoms of Feyland and become Empress of the Fey for nothing. She will not let you destroy her people – fey and human."

Logan raised his sword and slashed the air across Neriti's chest. The golden flash missed its target as Neriti used vampire speed to leaped over to stand before Jaegar, grabbing him by his wrist with the strength of a thousand vampire generals and pulling him towards the frosty wall of ice keeping Neriti, Logan, and Jaeger from entering Feyland. Before Jaegar could tear himself from her, she rammed his fist towards the wall.

Jaegar was prepared for the wall to shatter into tiny sharp shards of ice, but instead felt his elbow bend while the rest of his body caught up to his fist slamming against an impenetrable wall.

18

Kailin Gow

Pain. Intense electrifying pain shot through him as he felt the magic of the wall repel him back, sending him flying backwards through the air a hundred feet, along with Neriti, whose iron-tight grip on his wrist shackled him to her. The bones of his hand felt shattered. Disintegrated, turned into just skin and flesh.

"Mother effing!!!!" Jaegar howled, shaking his hand, trying to feel it as part of his body. The pain was excruciating, especially since there was a dead weight hanging onto his wrist cutting off all circulation. Jaegar grimaced, "Get off of me, you witch! What the hell were you doing?"

Neriti's eyes were closed. Her skin was no longer the color of life, but paler with a greenish tint. "I could feel it," she murmured. "Feyland magic. Your ring...on your hand, repelled us from crossing. You and I are Dark Fey. Your ring is not the Blood Ring. It is not the one I seek. Its magic did not grant us entrance into Feyland. It is an imposter ring, though it is made of Feyland crystal...where is the real Blood Ring?" she suddenly looked up at Jaegar with blood red anger in her eyes.

19

Blood Ring (Pulse #9)

"I don't know what ring you're talking about," Jaegar said.

"You found the cave...the one the ancient vampires were guarding..."

"Um, I still don't see what you're getting at," Jaegar said. "Speak human, not cryptic old world I-am-a-wise-old-wizard medieval talk. I spent a century trying to get rid of my medieval knight speak when I realized times had changed. Vampires who lived on and on must learn to adjust. I know you've just awakened from a thousand year sleep, so maybe if you'd assimilate yourself, you'd find you could get along with other vampires and maybe humans instead of being such a tightass."

Jaegar heard a chuckle, and saw Logan place the tip of his sword on the ground while leaning on the hilt. "Of all my years growing up as human, and hearing all about vampires from usual human tales like Bram Stoker's Dracula and those teen movies, I never thought a real one would be anything like you."

"Ha," Jaegar smirked. "Surprised you, did I? We come in all size and shapes. Like humans. We

were once human." Then Jaegar glanced over at
Neriti, whose eyes were still closed, her hand still in
an iron-grip on his wrist. Why won't she let go?

"Except that one," Logan said walking towards
them. "She was once fey, the Pixie Queen, green
blood, sharp teeth...the ones ruled by primitive
animalistic urges." Logan was almost to them. "Looks
like she's been as evil in the human lands here as
she was back in Feyland." Logan stopped walking
and fixed his eyes on the Wall of Ice as though he
could see beyond it. "As the new rulers of Feyland,
Breena and Kian would have to decide what to do
with her. We can't allow her, and anyone of fey blood
hurt the people in the Land Beyond the Crystal
River."

Jaegar looked into Logan's determined yet
earnest eyes. So the fey from Feyland were noble
beings... protecting the human race from evil, even
from their own, like the vampire guardians he,
Octavius, Stuart, and countless others who gave up
their lives fighting the likes of evil blood-thirsty
vampires like Mal fought as the Consortium. Jaegar
himself fought for selfish reasons...to preserve

humans for blood or the food source, and to protect the Life's Blood Carrier, whomever she would be, from the vampires who would drink her blood to gain incredible strength, immortality, yet uncontrollable rage and destructive powers. Why was the fey protecting the humans when they live literally in a different world?

As though Logan could read his mind, Logan said, "We can't let our own cause death and destruction in this human world. That's not what Breena would want with the incredible fey magic the fey possessed. She and I know this so well, and it is our mission to keep peace in Feyland, the peace we fought long and hard for, and even protect the Land Beyond the Crystal River, to ensure that peace. Breena and I know the struggles of the two worlds...for she was born to a human mother and a fey father, the King of Summer Court; while I was born to a human mother and a half fey, half-human father, the former King of the Wolf Fey."

"So you can easily cross back and forth from both worlds?" Jaegar asked. "But I, even though I am a so-called Dark Fey, can't?"

"That one, has a curse on her, a Blood Curse. She became a dark fey and condemn all her followers and offspring to the dark when she crossed over to the Land Beyond the Crystal River, found a human virgin girl whose beauty she envied and drained her of her blood, the blood that was blessed and protected by the girl's love, who was a human alchemist. I think, if I can remember fey history, all this took place during the medieval times of this world."

"That's partially what I knew of Neriti, too, but I thought it was all vampire lore, aimed to get vampires riled up thinking we are also magical beings instead of blood-thirsty killing monsters."

"So our fey lore adds up with vampire lore," Logan said. "And apparently, Feyland doesn't have to worry about her being able to come through the Wall of Ice. She may be able to look through, but she can't get through." Logan wiped his brow and muttered to himself. "Now I can finally go through and tell Breena and the others, the heightened danger here is resolved."

As if she had been listening and conscious the

entire time, Neriti quickly sprung back to life, with renewed energy. She looked wistfully through the clear section of the Wall of Ice seeing through all the frost, and seeing the twinkling lights amongst the trees, the two suns of Feyland floating in the lavender and vanilla sky, and the sweet melody of the grass. It was almost as though she was there, her former self, a fey, in the most beautiful land she had ever seen or experienced. Nothing in the Land Beyond the Crystal River could compare to its beauty...this land of enchantment. "If only I can go back...things would be different."

A bright white light flowed around her and Jaegar, burning with electricity and intense heat. "Ow...woman you are burning me up!" Jaegar tried to push her away, but her hand on Jaegar's wrist connecting her to him and the ring, tightened, involuntarily. "LET Go!" Jaegar pushed her again.

It was like the sun beating down on them, the Sun of the Earth that could burn vampires to a crisp. Jaegar's face contorted in panic and fear. Of all the years he spent walking the earth, he was going to die by burning to a crisp instead of staking.

Not what a knight like him would prefer since it was usually the cowardly way out for vampires...so he's always thought. He closed his eyes, ready for his body to ignite, while somewhere close to him, he can hear with his enhanced vampire hearing a soft but masculine voice talking as if through a long tunnel.

"I don't know what's happening, but this doesn't look good. Rose, it's Logan. I need your help. There's a kind of magic going on that your alchemist training can help explain, I think. The Dark Fey Queen, the Vampire Queen...she was turned through alchemy, wasn't she? If the fey lore was correct, the blood she took from the blessed maiden was enchanted by an alchemist so..."

Jaegar couldn't hear anymore, but now his eyes were wide open. Alchemy. Medicine. Science or even quackery. Like what the good old doctor from China tried to do with Life's Blood. Create vampire qualities in human so they can have the strength and power to fight them through Life's Blood...what Kalina was...a human whose veins flowed Life's Blood. Kalina was the only Carrier to achieve the doctor's goal...the only human who truly had vampire abilities and strength, yet was able to remain human. Perhaps she could be the key to all of this? Whatever key she was, Jaegar knew Kalina was still important to the fight against Neriti and the evil vampire minions she created. He missed her...so much his heart ached. Love. He tried so hard to stay away from Kal, to allow for her to figure out what she wanted, which she seemed to want Octavius, but try as he did, it seemed the fates would bring them back together. Or so he hoped.

There was a golden flash of light, and Jaegar thought Logan had used his sword again, but instead, a pretty red-head young woman in golden armor and wings, transparent wings like what...like a fairy, stood next to Logan. Jaegar blinked. A true fairy or fey as they call it here.

"Rose," Logan said. He looked adoringly at her for a brief second before turning serious. "Over there...there she is and..."

Neriti pulled Jaegar in for a full embrace, enveloping him more in the electrifying burning heat. He thought he was going to melt now. He let out a

26

yell before he saw a bright white light explode before him with a small burst of golden light following. But it was too late.

Chapter 2

He could feel air rushing past him, hard, stinging, but cold air, as though he was flying at full speed, as he frequently traveled as a vampire.

The ice cold air was refreshing against his scorched heated skin. Thank God he wasn't going to be burning for all eternity. Was he truly dead? Did he finally escaped his vampirism by dying?

He opened his eyes.

Wham!

Just in time.

His body was hurtling down like a torpedo through the air and through the clouds, headed straight towards the jagged sharp snowcapped mountain tops that jutted out amongst the sea of white frothy mist. He turned with all the strength he had, feeling the weight of death on his shoulders, and narrowly missed one rocky peak, while he continued his nose-dive down to the green valley below.

"I feel like death," Jaegar muttered to himself. "My strength is so drained, and it feels like it's taking every effort of mine to move, like I'm weighed down by bricks, by Death himself."

"Shut up you pion!"

"Whaah?" Jaegar looked up and saw the beautiful yet detestable face of Kalina's ancestor...

"Get off me, you Ass!" Jaegar shouted before plunging down into a spread of leafy green treetops, densely packed together like brussel sprouts on a mountaintop.

"I should have expected your landing would be sloppy and out of control, unbefitting the strength of an ancient vampire." That voice, laced with sarcasm and condescension. Who else could it be but the ancient she-bitch Queen Neriti.

She lay sprawled out next to him, having tumbled off him and on top of another treetop. "Who knew I would have a leech riding my back the entire time I was freefalling. No wonder why I felt like death. The Mother of it was on my back."

Neriti turned towards him, her eyes

smoldering with anger. "How dare you talk to your superior this way. You should be honored I rode on your back. Octavius your general was beyond delight when I would even look upon him with desire."

"Um, that's because you compelled him," Jaegar said in disgust. "How pathetic."

"The pathetic one is you," Neriti said through clenched teeth. "You can't seem to stop spewing idiotic thoughts and words all this time, even when you were transported. 'I miss my Kal. Why didn't Kal pick me?' Like I thought. You are an idiot through and through."

"And you," Jaegar said with clenched teeth, "Is the bigger idiot. You brought all this on yourself...and created an entire race of vampires doomed to the dark forever. Human lives destroyed. Vampire lives destroyed. No wonder why the Wall of Ice repelled you. No wonder why this ring threw you and me as far away as possible from the gate into Feyland. For you to think you even have a chance to get back in, for God knows what reason besides your usual motto – 'To take over the world, um, worlds, plural', you are the biggest fool. Give it up now."

"You will eat your words, minion. My will is like iron. I am the Queen of Everything! I will rule the worlds, and I will destroy all who stand in my way to that goal. I will lie, cheat, kill, maim, bully, use sorcery, dark magic, compulsion, calling of dark spirits, demons, blackmail, taint the reputations of innocents, seek out and stalk those who dare stand up to me, brainwash the minds of idealistic youths to do the dirty work and slandering of my rivals for me, and I will instruct my agents of deception to spread rumors against my enemies; I will use the goodwill of Christ-like men to spread my evil influence and message of hate through their media and films. I will manipulate. I will bash. I will do everything I can to provoke and promote this evil, like a barracuda intent on devouring all the fish around me. In other words, Simpleton, I will destroy everyone who dare stand in my way, especially that copycat Kalina. She is the one I pledged to take down and destroy. I have sent word to all my minions, my agents, and even spies who are now closing in on Kalina to act as her friends and confidants; to do everything to destroy her. She is the one I hate the most, for daring to be

31

like me, for sharing my likeness, for winning the love I so crave...from Octavius, from the vampires, from all...it should be me who is most loved, most popular, not that copycat, that wannabe..."

Jaegar had enough. He raised his hand to shove it into the witch's mouth, trying to stop the flow of hate spewing from her soul. It didn't matter how much pain his hand was in, having been shattered by the Wall of Ice earlier before, but now having Neriti's sharp fangs clamped down hard on it, biting it deep he was certain, she would tear off chunks of his flesh. And gobble it down.

By being struck by the ring's white light and energy, Neriti's black hair was tainted by a chunk of white hair in front, giving her a look like an old hag, and a demon. For a second, Jaegar thought he saw black leather bat-like wings extend from her back as her hair plastered back on her skull and her eyes turned blood red. The Monster. This was Neriti's true form as a vampire...not the beautiful youthful woman resembling Kalina, but the blood-thirsty one of lore. Dracula's version. Nosferatu.

Her feet became claws, her hands became

claws. She was like an enormous bat, but now her skin was changing. Instead of fur like a bat's, she was developing scales, black scales that covered her face and then the rest of her. Her arms became thicker, like tree trunks and longer until they were like her hind legs, and she fell forward on all fours. Her nose and mouth elongated into a muzzle and a mouth filled with rows of jagged teeth.

Jaegar's eyes nearly fell out of his socket. He had never seen this before. Worse yet, his hand was still in this ghastly creature's mouth.

He wrenched his hand out, seeing the flesh of is thumb torn off.

At last, the transformation of Neriti to this creature stopped. As though by him removing his hand from her mouth, he made it stopped. He looked at his bloodied stump of a hand and knew why. The ring was glowing. Through the magic within that ring, Neriti had now transformed into a hideous creature, her true monster form...and that was not of an enormous black leather bat, but of a black-scaled dragon.

"A black dragon!" shouts from below on the

ground rose up to Jaegar. In his shock, he had forgotten where he was...on the top of trees in some mountainside. Below was some kind of ancient village with stone sidewalks and dirt roads. Then he saw the porcelain tiled rooftops of the worn out village buildings. They looked familiar, very familiar as though he'd been there before.

The smell of boiling dumpling and noodles filled the air, along with steamed buns sold on the streets by poor village vendors. Jaegar smiled. He knew this place well. It was the ancient Chinese village he and Kal, Octavius, Stuart, Max, and even Justin fought the Life's Blood turned vampire army. It was the village where the good old Chinese doctor who experimented with Life's Blood lived. But something was different. When they fought here, the village was abandoned for years, desecrated by time. But now...it was brimming with life and activity as though it was an earlier period of time...

"Are you sure you saw a black dragon?" another voice asked. "If you have, it is bad. Bad luck."

"I hope not then, but I saw a black winged

34

creature with red eyes and sharp teeth."

"A bat perhaps," the villager said.

"It couldn't be, not the size of this one," the second villager said.

"Perhaps it is one of those monsters who have been stealing our people and drinking their blood...we have to put a stop to it. With those monsters around, it is not safe to go out at night."

"I hear those monsters resemble people and then when they bare their fangs, they become monsters."

Neriti the black dragon, raised her head and shot her red gaze down to follow the voices below. She drew up her wings, flapping it like a great black hideous bird.

"Oh, there it is again!" the first villager's voice shouted excitedly. "High up there in those trees."

Neriti raised her head and let out a roar, shooting out a line of fire into the sky.

Jaegar was stunned. She had transformed herself truly into the beast, complete with the fire and steaming nostrils. No wonder why when she held him, the heat from her body, had been burning him up. Or could the ring with whatever fey magic it had transformed her, while transported her to this village, along with him...the ring's wearer?

Was this truly the magical Blood Ring she was seeking and it had sensed the evil in her so strongly that it reacted this way to her? Even through him, the power of the ring affected her with such strength of magic, neither she nor he could resist it.

"That fire! That smoke! It can't be a bat!" the second villager shouted. "It is one of those fabled monsters. The winged beast that breathed fire. The dragon. A black dragon, no less."

"What's so special about a black dragon?" the first villager asked.

"Don't you know? In the western world they are demons. They are bad...they bring death and destruction to many."

"But here, in China?"

"It is mixed, good or bad. They say the dragons must be appeased in order to be protected from them, but if you do not offer up offerings, they will cause famine and diseases...this black dragon has the eyes of the devil. I get the feeling..."

36

With a swoop down the trees, Neriti grabbed the villager in her talons, raised it to her large mouth, opening to its full size, which reeked of sulfur, brimstone, and decaying raw flesh.

"Have mercy!" the villager cried out.

Wooden arrows from the remaining villager pelted the scaly skin of the dragon, bouncing off its black armor. Five more men with pick axes, swords, and hatchets joined the villager by charging at the dragon.

"We will not let you bring your evil and destruction into our village," the tallest and most muscular of the villagers said, wielding a sword and jumping high up on top of the dragon's head. "Not only have you attacked one of our people, but you dare set foot into our lands blaring your fangs, fire, and talons as an invader. I have no doubt you do not come here in peace. Now let go of Shao Feng right now or I won't chop your head off!"

Neriti's claws clamped down harder on the young man within until he began screaming in pain.

"Looks like you chose the second path," the swordsman said. "Prepare to die!" He swung his sword wide and planted it into the dragon's neck, slicing it down to the bone, causing it to drop the first villager to the ground.

She turned her head and tried to scorch him with her fire, but ended up hitting Jaegar who ducked out of the way by hiding behind a tree. The fire singed his hair and burned off his jeans, black t-shirt, and leather jacket. "Great, now I'm naked," Jaegar threw up his hands and ducked behind some trees, moving along the trees to gather some leaves to cover up his privates.

The swordsman leaped from a limb on a tree to land on the dragon's head, but Neriti shook it violently until he fell off and landed on her back. He struck down on her back with his sword and grazed her shoulders.

With a roar, Neriti swung her tail towards her back, knocking the swordsman to the ground.

"We'll get the beast, Doctor," the young kung fu master with an ax, said. "You should rest...you need your strength...with your experiments..."

"I am the mayor of this village, Ming. It is my duty to protect everyone here..."

"No, rest, Doctor," the young man with a tattoo of a tiger on his arm came over to lift the doctor. "That fall from the dragon's back was steep. You could have internal injuries."

"I am alright, Fu Long." the Doctor said. "I am a martial arts master after all. I pledge to protect this village when you all chose me as the mayor. I cannot let the people down."

"But Doctor...your work, it is more important than what goes on at this village. It can change all of humankind. We need you to find a cure..." Ming said. "Leave it to Fu and me. We can slay this dragon like those knights you hear about from the west. And..." Ming stopped talking in mid-sentence, his mouth hanging open as his eyes widened in disbelief.

Fighting the dragon, dressed in traditional Chinese villager cotton robe with drawstring pants, in all white, was a very handsome man with blue eyes and black hair that fell down to his shoulders. It was not tied up into a bun at the top or back of his head as was the fashion of the men from the village. He was clearly not from the village, yet he was holding a sword forged from the village, and fighting the dragon in a style that could be consider medieval European.

Ming, Fu Long, and the doctor shook their heads. What was a medieval knight doing here along with a black dragon? Could he have followed the dragon to this village? Why was the knight wearing a Chinese attire?

Kailin Gow

Chapter 3

Jaegar was in his element. After all these years since being turned into a vampire, he was a knight again. He had wandered into the village while the kung fu master fought Neriti and had entered into a large well-furnished, well-kept household, along with servants and a pond filled with red, orange, and white carp. The house looked familiar at first so Jaegar didn't feel at all uncomfortable or self-conscious walking in. Upon being seen by the young ladies who appeared to be maids or servants of the household, they would giggle and look down, averting their eyes for a bit to avoid looking at his leaf-clad body.

He gestured to them about finding clothes, and they pointed to one of the rooms. He walked through the hallway to the room they pointed to and entered to find a large wardrobe filled with men's clothing. He chose the all white attire and some socks and shoes before walking down to another room where he found a chest full of weapons and swords. Whoever owned this house must be doing pretty well, Jaegar thought. He picked out a sword and tested it. Light, sharp, yet sturdy; it was a fine sword.

He was going to end Neriti with this sword, if he could do it today. He saw the look in her eyes. He heard her heartfelt speech about ruling the world and destroying everyone in her path, especially Kalina. He could not stand aside and let this Queen of Bullies, the Queen of Mean destroy everything good and decent in this world. Through Kalina's love, he had discovered what it meant to live, what it meant to have meaning and a purpose in this existence he had. He must fight her with as much as he'd got. Even if it ended here.

At least he would have died a knight, once again. And this time, he would have died slaying a dragon.

Jaegar walked faster through the hallways towards the fight outside in the forests near the village. Yet, his feet was taking him elsewhere...the ring was taking him elsewhere. What was with this ring? It was as if by touching the ring to the Wall of Ice, it had been activated with some sort of magic.

As he walked, more memory came to him, of this place, of the village. He knew he was here before during that battle where Stuart almost died, where Justin almost died, where Octavius almost died, where Kalina...Yes, that battle where they were outnumbered by Life's Blood vampires and ambushed. The odds were impossible, yet they won.

Here. In this house. Years later. Hundreds of years later. In the doctor's house, the one who created Life's Blood.

"So this is the good doctor's house," Jaegar muttered to himself. And that brave swordsman...he is the doctor who would create the rare blood that would eventually flow fully and purely in Kalina's blood. Oh how he owed much to this human. He would have to protect him at all costs.

Especially since the good doctor has yet in this time of his life, to discover Life's Blood...a fact certainly Neriti would have figured out.

When Neriti had wished to go back, while

holding onto Jaegar's wrist, connecting herself to the ring who had repelled her, it was not to go back in time to when she first became a vampire. She did not regret that, apparently, but to the time she met the doctor and compelled him to create Life's Blood using her blood.

By wishing to go back in time to before knowing the good doctor as a vampire, she was going to kill him in order to prevent the line of Life's Blood Carriers to live, including Kalina.

Jaegar clenched his fists tighter. How he could not stand this woman, Neriti. How he wanted to ground her down to the dirt. She was ruthless enough and heartless enough to go after and destroy everyone around Kalina even to the point of planning to kill the good doctor and destroy his village.

"Bacca!" Jaegar yelled, "Feng dan!" "Fool!" He called Neriti a fool over and over again first in Japanese, Chinese, and English.

Then he rushed out with sword blazing on his mission to slay this damn effing dragon.

Chapter 4

Knights were bound by the Code of Chivalry. Jaegar had been a knight in England when he was turned by mercy by the Roman General Octavius. His brother Stuart was preparing to become a priest, yet both brothers including their father were turned so they would survive the plague. To Stuart, it was a fate worse than death, to walk the Earth as a blood-thirsty monster.

"Thank God, he was the one Kalina loved," Jaegar said. "Well, she had enough love for him to turn him human." And that one time her blood was forced down his throat, turning him into a violent Life's Blood crazed vampire... that could have been proof she loved Octavius or Stuart more than him. But when she gave freely of her blood that one time when she risked her life to sequestered herself with him in his Life's Blood crazed condition, that one time he fell so much deeper in love with her he would gladly give his life for her, he drank her blood given in love, and he became gloriously and miraculously a human. He knew she did love him enough. He knew she had always loved him, but he had walked away from it, taken on his duty to protect her with all his strength and might. So...he asked Octavius to turn him back into a vampire so he could have that strength. He did it because he loved the lady he protected so much, he could forever be her knight. He even asked Octavius to keep his second turning into a vampire a secret from Kalina.

"Talk about being a chivalrous fool," Jaegar said to himself. "I take the cake for following the Code of Chivalry, don't I? Guess you could say I'm the most noble of them all?" He smirked and shook his head smiling. He had no regrets in being Kalina's knight.

Now he could die in peace, having fought and lived his hardest for the most worthy cause of all...to save humankind by protecting and saving the woman who holds the key to stopping the vampire queen Neriti.

He flew into the air, while the dragon was thrashing its tail, knocking down trees while shooting streams of fire from its mouth, aimed at innocent people and buildings in the village. She had set a patch of trees in the forest on fire, injuring the birds and animals residing there.

The kung fu master with the hatchet was hacking away at the dragon's legs, which were like thick tree trunks lined with iron scales. His hatchet bounced off, barely making a dent.

"Oh come on," Jaegar yelled to the dragon Neriti, "Pick on someone with your own blood type...none...and stop harassing these poor villagers."

He brought down his sword on her back, hitting the wounds the good doctor had sliced open, and driving his sword deeper. "Good doctor also is a masterful swordsman. I'm impressed."

Neriti bucked up in pain, roaring and spewing flames into the trees nearby. Jaegar held on with one hand he had plunged deeply into her back while the other, the one with the ring, held the sword. His hand had healed quickly after he compelled one of the servant girls at the doctor's house to offer up some of her blood. He needed it badly and was so famished, he nearly drank her to death, but stopped. He apologized and gave her a fresh red rose when he left, compelling her to forget everything.

With a wide swing he tried to lope off her head, but Neriti turned just in time to blow a blast of heated air before it became flames at Jaegar, who had to leap off of her back and to the ground.

He landed on his feet near the good doctor, who was instructing people with buckets of water where to put out the fires. The village was blazing up in flames, along with the forest. Women, children, and elderly men were all lending a hand to bring bowls, cups, buckets, pitchers, or whatever container they could find to fill up with water to put out the fire.

Jaegar saw a little girl in pigtails, around four years old, carrying a porcelain bowl of water over to an elderly man to pour over the rooftop of one of the buildings.

The second time around, she nearly tripped on her own feet, almost dropping the bowl when Jaegar caught her and steadied the bowl in her hands. "Good work," Jaegar said, patting her head. She looked up at Jaegar and smiled a crooked smile, her front baby teeth barely there. Jaegar couldn't help himself. He pulled her in for a hug. So warm. So alive. He was filled with a sudden longing deep within him. What would it be like to have a little one like this one? To have a daughter who would look up to him with a crooked but happy smile despite all the chaos going on around him? Could he even wish for such happiness when he was a vampire?

"Thank you, Uncle," the little girl smiled back up at him, running clumsily back to fill her bowl with water, to begin again.

"I am Uncle Jaegar," he said. "What's your name?"

"Shin Shin," the little girl proudly said.

"Like the word 'star'," Jaegar asked.

The girl nodded.

Jaegar kissed her forehead tenderly. "You are one, little Shin Shin. You are doing such a good job! Just be careful not to get burned."

"I will be careful," the little girl said. "Bye bye Uncle Jaegar. You be careful too." She smiled so happily, her eyes looked like tiny smiles.

Blood Ring (Pulse #9)

Jaegar pulled her in for another hug. He wished he could hold onto this feeling of happiness for a while longer.

He tightened his hug and then pulled away letting her go on her merry way.

"You have a way with children," the Doctor Swordsman said next to him. "It is a good thing you were so gentle with my daughter just now or I would have stake you, Vampire."

Jaegar almost leaped back but remained calm. "So Shin Shin is your daughter?"

"Yes," the doctor said smiling proudly. "I should stake you for being a vampire, but I sense something different about you. What is it?"

"I have been changed by the love of a good woman," Jaegar laughed.

"A human woman?" the doctor asked.

Jaegar nodded.

"Just like us human men," the doctor said. "Shin Shin's mother tamed my rage and demons. If it was not for her, I would not have become a doctor nor mayor of this town, San Ten."

50

"Heaven's Mountain," Jaegar suddenly knew the translation from somewhere within him.

"Yes, Heaven's Mountain. We are one of the villages closest to the clouds." He leaned in as though he was about to whisper. "We started this village years ago up in the mountains so we can find solace, so that we can train, practice our martial arts, and live a peaceful life. We are all, from Fu Long to Ming, to myself...former imperial officers and guards of the Empress. Before then, I was a lone swordsman, who made a living finding bounty. I was not proud of what I did, but I was at a bad time of my life until I met the woman who would become my wife. Then things changed..." The doctor smiled.

"I know what you mean," Jaegar said. He looked over to see that the fires were slowly but surely being put out, thanks to the remarkable teamwork everyone in the village had.

"Now," the doctor said, flexing his shoulders and stretching out. "It seems the fires will be extinguished soon." He picked up his sword and rushed out towards the forest where Neriti was fighting four of the kung fu masters. The doctor glanced back, "I must go join my brothers to take down this dragon. I trust you will behave yourself, Vampire, amongst my people...or..."

"No need to worry about what I'll do when you're off fighting the dragon, Doc," Jaegar said, picking up his sword and rushing quickly up to the doctor in record speed. "I'm going to fight that dragon with you."

The doctor looked at him, "Who's going to look out for Shin Shin then? She's counting on you to help her if she stumbles." He smiled.

Jaegar was taken aback. No one in his entire existence as a vampire had ever trusted him with a human child or in Shin Shin's case, more like a baby than a child. He was a vampire after all.

"Thank you for your kindness and your ability to give me the benefit of a doubt. I know you are wary of my kind, which you have a right to (and you should teach Shin Shin to be careful around vampires, too) but I have a score to settle with that witch. She is the Vampire Queen turned into a hideous dragon. She is the worse, most evil vampire who ever existed, killing countless of humans and vampires alike. She is the most ruthless and remorseless psychotic predator around. I heard her declaration to rule not only all humankind but all of the supernatural and magical realms. And..." Jaegar gritted his teeth, "She specifically wants to kill my girl Kalina and destroy everyone and everything close to her. Dear doctor..."

"Shaw," he said. "Just call me Shaw."

"Shaw," Jaegar said. "I am afraid you and your village were attacked by this Queen Neriti because of Kalina."

The doctor's brow furrowed in confusion. "How? What would I know about Kalina?"

Jaegar took a deep breath and said, "I am from the future time. It's hard to explain and we don't have much time, but you have to survive this. You have to live. Your work with the vampires will be very important, crucial even, to the future of humankind and vampires, especially Kalina. Kalina is...your Masterpiece. She is the one who will fulfill your vision of a future where humans can exist peacefully with vampires."

The doctor stumbled back, as if he just had a

53

heart attack. Jaegar caught him and held him up.

"Easy now, Shaw. It is a lot to take in, but it is true. I don't know how it happened, but I fought here in your village, in your house, hundreds of years later against some strong and ruthless vampires. It was one of our most costly battles."

"My house? Hundreds of years in the future?" the doctor shook his head. "How was it? Is it as it is now?"

Jaegar shook his head. Now having met the doctor and knowing how much he cared for and protected his village, it would be heartbreaking for him to know his village became an abandoned ghost town when Jaegar, Kalina, and the gang came upon it He wanted to tell him the truth, but the look on the doctors face...concern, worry, and vulnerability made Jaegar said, "Just as it is now."

The doctor was about to fight the most heartless of creatures, the most evil and vile of creatures ever lived...Neriti. He needed to have hope that his fight will be for the betterment of his people's future.

"Good," the doctor said. "Hopefully by then,

54

everyone's home will have proper addresses display on their walls." He chuckled.

Jaegar chuckled along with him. Loyal as loyal could be, the doctor was a knight as well, worrying about the details of his village. Having been the Empress' guardian once. He and the doctor understood each other well. Two soldiers who were trained to stand up and fight and never give up.

Together they charged, raising their swords above them as they jumped up onto the dragon's belly, slashing into the unprotected area at the same time. No black scales covered the soft underbelly of the dragon allowing for Shaw and Jaegar's swords to cut deep enough until Neriti bellowed out in pain.

With her talons, she tried to swipe away the irritating gnats beneath her. She was far more powerful than a mere minion second-rate vampire and a human doctor. Even before she transformed into a hideous black dragon, she was the strongest queen of them all. No one in this mortal human land can withstand her power. It took all of the Vampire Consortium, Octavius, the strong and mighty vampire Samson, and an army of vampires to finally put her into her tomb for a long sleep, hidden away from humankind and vampires for centuries. How could these two dare to think they can defeat her?

"Quick!" Jaegar shouted to the doctor, get off the ground or her massive heft would stomp on you!"

The doctor leaped up onto the top of a tree opposite another treetop Jaegar was perched on, catching his breath while his kung fu brothers attacked Neriti from the sides. "Her sheer size and fire power can topple our entire village. I am only human, albeit a masterful swordsman, but sooner or later, like my kung fu brothers, I will lose energy."

"I don't know what made her transformation into a dragon," Jaegar said. "It must be tied to this ring I'm wearing. The fey power of this ring reacted to her, using me as a conduit."

The doctor leaped over the branches to join Jaegar on his treetop to look at his ring. "May I?" He held out his hand.

Jaegar took the ring off and dropped it into the doctor's palm. It landed softly like a normal ring.

The doctor looked carefully at the ring, observing it in close detail. Without warning, he pulled Jaegar's hand up, then his sword and cut Jaegar's palm.

"Hey! Hey! Machete, what are you doing?" Jaegar pulled his hand back and away from the doctor.

"Just one drop of your blood. Please." The doctor gestured towards he ring.

Jaegar got it. He gave the doctor his palm, and the doctor lifted his hand where a drop of blood fell onto the ring.

The ring jumped, sizzled and sparked from the raw contact of Jaegar's blood before absorbing it in and becoming the clear crystal in the center.

"Um, what was that?" Jaegar asked.

"It appeared the ring is tied to you or the essence from your blood," Shaw said. He placed the ring back onto Jaegar's finger. "Now think about what you would like to do to this twig I am holding. How would you like to see it being used?"

Jaegar thought it was a ridiculous exercise at first but he concentrated and focused. The twig combusted into flames.

"Whoa!" Jaegar said. "That was exactly what I

was thinking." He held up his hand to look at the ring. "You mean because this ring is connected to me somehow, it has given me some kind of magical powers? Like what the fey has? OhMyGod! What a trip. Never would I have imagined having this kind of power. No vampire can." His eyes widen with excitement as he looked at the doctor. "So everything that's happened to Neriti...it's because I wished it?"

The doctor shrugged. "You tell me. Did you wish for her to turn into a dragon?"

"Not exactly," Jaegar said. "She was really getting on my nerves, grabbing hold of my hand to try to punch it through that Wall of Ice. I did not want that witch to go through. Because, according to that Wolf Prince, if she does, she will become more powerful and more ruthless. I've seen what she's done in this mortal land. I can imagine what she would do if she entered the land of the fey. They're peaceful creatures...she will take full advantage of them. So I will myself to pull back. I will the wall to repel us, to turn solid and impenetrable. Man," Jaegar stopped and looked around. "It is true. Whatever I wished for, worked on Neriti. I didn't exactly wanted her to turn into a dragon, but I wanted her to see herself in her raw dark self and not the beautiful young woman whom she resembled as she walked around pretending to be human."

Jaegar clenched his jaws. "She has my beloved Kalina's face. She looks like her, yet she isn't her, and it was so hard for me to fight succumbing to her evilness when she looked like Kalina."

"I see," the doctor said. "So she was turned into this dragon because of you."

"Uh huh," Jaegar said. "And I'm beginning to see how we can defeat this bitch."

"Ready when you are, sorcerer!" Shaw said, raising his sword. "Just don't turn it into something worse..."

Jaegar grabbed his sword and landed on top of the dragon's head. "It's time you head back home, away from here, you sneaky snake. You used me and the connection I had to this ring to snake your way back in time to try to kill off the doctor who would discover Life's Blood, thus preventing Kalina from ever becoming a Life's Blood Carrier. I've had it with your lies, manipulations, and deceit. Take us back

59

home, now!" He struck the palm of his hand with his ring hard on the dragon's head where sparks flew and a blinding white light exploded around him. A burning electrifying sensation heated around him, as before when they had traveled back in time. They were moving...Neriti and him, through the air at record speed, away from the village and the good people who lived there. Jaegar waved, hoping to catch a glimpse of Shaw or Shin Shin, but he was already far away in time and space.

Chapter 5

Jaegar felt a pang of loss. They felt almost like family to him. Was it because Kalina's blood was from the mixture of this doctor's blood? He discovered Life's Blood and legend had it that his daughter...Shin Shin was the first to succeed in becoming a Life's Blood Carrier, thus falling in love with a vampire from France and giving her Life's Blood to him for him to become human.

No wonder he felt such a connection to the doctor and Shin Shin. They were Kalina and Max's ancestors.

And Neriti...she was no longer a black dragon, but a large black raven with blood red eyes.

"Not at all what I was thinking, but it will do," Jaegar said. "You are still your miserable true form...ravens are ill-omen and carriers of murdered souls. Wait...I was thinking something along that line...that someone as heartless as you should feel the sting of your crimes...all those murdered souls you heartlessly slaughtered – humans, fey, and vampires alike. If it was not for you, I would never have become a vampire, doomed to crave the blood of all those poor souls that I..." Jaegar turned away and swallowed. He had never been hit with such guilt before, such an intense burden that weighed down his bones. He thought of Shin Shin and the doctor... despite the kindness of the doctor and pure innocence the sweet child Shin Shin had, Jaegar somehow was able to read the thoughts of the doctor for one brief moment when the doctor first approached him. He was deciding whether to stake him or not, while a painful memory flashed through his mind. Little Shin Shin was motherless; and Shaw was a widower because of a vampire who violently fought and killed the beautiful woman warrior.

If a vampire or anyone had killed the woman Jaegar loved so violently like the images that flashed in his head; he would never trust any vampire again. He would hate all vampires. He would be so filled with rage that he would make it a mission to hunt down that vampire in revenge.

Shaw could've tried to stake him but he didn't. He could have shown him hate, but he shown him acceptance and kindness. Jaegar was so intent on getting to fight Neriti that he didn't grasp the full meaning of the doctor's acceptance of him.

And now Jaegar was hit with the most profound feeling of all – all those he had killed, all those he had drank their blood to death...to him they used to be merely food for a vampire, but now, he realized they were people with souls, loves, and lives. They had families, children maybe, dogs and pets who loved and depended on them; yet he and many of his kind heartlessly and cruelly slaughtered them. Just like their cruel Vampire Queen had led them to become...murderers, bullies, and senseless attackers.

"That is why you are a raven now," Jaegar said to Neriti. "Through the power of this ring, you will get a taste of your own medicine. You will carry the burden of all those murdered souls around you until you can feel what it is to be merciful."

"Caw caw!" Neriti crowed. "But I was never human like you or any other vampire, fool. I will never understand the humanity you all hold dear."

"You can speak?" Jaegar asked. "But…"

"Ravens are smarter than you think, you fool. Of course I can speak."

"Even when you were a dragon, you could speak?"

"I could hear, too, fool," Neriti said. "I heard your conversation with the doctor…about the ring. It does everything you wish it to, does it?"

"Perhaps," Jaegar said, suddenly on guard. Neriti must not get this ring.

"Wish me back to my former form, fool!" Neriti commanded.

"Fine. You will become a hideous black dragon again, complete with bad breath and itchy skin."

"No! My form as a young woman, imbecile!" Neriti crowed.

"I liked you better this way," Jaegar said. "Do you feel the remorse, raven? Do you feel anything in that stone cold heart of yours?"

Neriti laughed. "I told you, I was never human nor was I of this world."

"Yes, you're from Feyland, but I met Logan,

and he seemed like a decent and normal guy, yet he's fey. Perhaps, it's not where you're from that is the excuse you used to be this ruthless, cold-hearted monster. Perhaps, witch, it is just you."

Neriti made a sudden rolling turn, throwing Jaegar nearly off her back, and grasped Jaegar with her claws. "You don't know anything, fool!" she screamed into his face.

Jaegar closed his eyes while enduring the stream of spit and warm bad breath pelted at him.

The raven folded her wings around Jaegar like an iron-clad prison and dove down into a freefall.

"Hey hey, what are you doing?" Jaegar cried, struggling to get out of her prison.

"Turn me back now or I will squash you like a bug."

"So squash me like a bug," Jaegar said casually.

"You fool!" Neriti cried. "You are nothing like Octavius. No wonder Kalina chose him. You are more like an adolescent than a man! Sure you may be a pleasurable toy for the time-being, but women want a man they can feel like a woman with."

Blood Ring (Pulse #9)

"Like Octavius," Jaegar said, feeling a bit of jealousy at his old friend and general. "Kalina made her choice."

"No, she didn't, fool!" Neriti shouted at him, spewing spit and bad breath. "You left her, you came chasing after me, leaving her behind to be with Octavius. You made that choice for her, fool, and I mean you are truly a fool if you haven't seen that." Neriti wrapped her wings around Jaegar tighter, squeezing the life out of him. "Change me now or I really will squash you, and then I will let you splattered all over the earth."

"Perhaps this is a just atonement for all I've done," Jaegar said.

"Fool! Fool! Fool!" Neriti crowed over and over again. The ground was quickly approaching, and if she did not stop, they would both be splattered all over the earth. She could squash him like she threatened, but she needed his ring. Maybe she didn't need him wearing the ring, then she could get rid of this albatross hanging around her neck. His pathetic vampire guilt and those wailing murdered souls' voices were pounding into her head as though she would explode.

The ground was now within sight. Buildings, houses, concrete sidewalks. And there far in the distance down the same street but at a park was a young woman with long dark hair and chocolate eyes fighting off a large vampire man.

"Kalina," Neriti whispered.

Jaegar immediately sprung to life, touched his ring, and said, "Change back to your human not-so-scary form, raven...or you'll scare the living daylights out of these people."

Neriti could feel her wings retracting and her claws become hands, while her head grow smaller, and her body adjusted itself upright. Soon, she was her former self, the face that looked like Kalina's.

She floated down through the air, grabbing some clothing from a washing line from one of the buildings and slipping it on quickly. She landed in front of Kalina and stared angrily at her.

"So copycat, I'm back here again in your world where everyone loves you."

Kalina blocked a punch from the vampire she was fighting and grabbed his wrist, pulling him in close where she quickly staked him. He crumbled into a pile of dust in front of them. "I can't exactly welcome you back with open arms, could I?" Kalina asked. "I hate you back, too...especially for killing Jaegar."

"Who said she killed me?" a familiar deep and sultry male voice said from behind Kalina.

Kalina turned her head slowly, without losing sight of the tricky and manipulative Neriti who would be glad for any distractions so she could easily drain Kalina of her blood.

"Jae..." his name hung in mid-air as Jaegar crushed her mouth with his, kissing her long and deeply, his tongue tasting hers while his fingers ran through her silky soft hair that smell like jasmine and lavender.

"Kal," Jaegar whispered softly while gazing deeply into her eyes. "I thought I'd never see you again."

"Me too," Kalina's voice broke. "We looked everywhere for you and couldn't find you. We saw vampire dust everywhere. You weren't there. You left your Life's Blood ring behind...the one I made for you. You'd never take that off. You couldn't unless you had turned to dust. You'd never leave that behind. You'd never leave me behind...Jaegar."

Kalina's cheeks were wet with tears, and Jaegar pulled her in closer to him, kissing away her tears. "Oh Kalina, Kalina," he whispered over and over again as he kissed her hair, her eyelids, and her mouth. "I wanted to be the noble knight for you. I wanted to keep you safe forever. I thought that you and Oct..."

"Will you look at that?" Neriti sneered. "The lovebirds have united. It seems, Octavius, the most precious girl in your life prefers another."

Kalina and Jaegar looked up to see Octavius standing at the far end of the field. He was dressed in a dark tailored Armani suit, a white shirt, and a blue tie that matched the tint in his eyes. His arms were crossed while he took in the scene.

"General Octavius," Neriti said, almost with a sigh. "You are still a sight to behold. Have you come to rejoin my army?"

Octavius barely acknowledged Neriti as he strode pass her towards Kalina.

Blood Ring (Pulse #9)

"Kalina, I came as soon as I could. As you can see, I just got out of a meeting and..."

Kalina smiled happily at Octavius, which made the horrendous trip he had just undertaken to get from Beverly Hills to China using vampire speed and flight, worth it. He haven't seen her smile like that for weeks since they buried Jaegar. But there he was now, hugging Kalina with such love in his eyes. "Jaegar's alive!" she cried, going over to hug Octavius. "We didn't lose him."

"Octavius," Jaegar smiled.

"Happy you are with us," Octavius said, patting Jaegar's back. "You couldn't have been resurrected at a more timely hour."

Jaegar looked around. "Why? What's going on?"

"Kalina?" Octavius asked, looking to her.

Kalina looked at Octavius and then Jaegar. "Octavius, I called you here because there have been reports from some of the Life's Blood Carriers that the vampires they have turned back to humans through their Life's Blood, are turning back to vampires."

Chapter 6

Jaegar shook his head in disbelief. "Come again?"

"We already know Life's Blood turned vampires to humans have been reverting back to vampires in some cases, but now all of them?" Octavius asked.

"I've been tracking all the cases, getting each Life's Blood Carrier to report to me which vampires they've turned. I also have been keeping records and researching the history and ancestry of Life's Blood Carriers before Max, and who did they turned," Kalina said. "Justin's been taking samples of their blood and analyzing them to see which strain is causing the turned vampires to revert back. I thought it was just a few cases, but now, it seems slowly each one will at one point or another."

"You mean when the vampires are turned by Life's Blood, they are humans temporarily?" Jaegar asked.

Blood Ring (Pulse #9)

"Permanently and temporarily," Kalina said. "They are like werewolves in that they are humans but shift into wolves. Well, these vampires, through Life's Blood, become human again, only to shift into vampires."

"So you've found some a group of dangerous, rogue vampires preying on the Life's Blood Carriers here?" Octavius asked. He patted Kalina on the head, proud of his spunky courageous yet fiercely beautiful and proud woman. She was the bravest human he had ever known, and he had known many generals and fighters.

"No one harms my sisters," Kalina said gritting her teeth. "I will take down each and every one of those rogue vampires."

"Are they connected to those Life's Blood turned vampires?" Octavius asked.

"This group appears to be," Kalina said. "I don't understand, though. Why would a Life's Blood turned vampire who was now human, become vicious out-of-control vampires when they returned to their vampire state?"

"They could not help it?" Jaegar said. "All that

pent up energy, then that frustration of having turned human just to become a vampire again...it can drive a vampire crazy. They have all the good and bad of both."

Kalina was looking at him as though a light bulb had gone off in her head. "That's right! Jaegar you would know. I turned you human once, but it didn't work. You reverted back to being a vampire but only a permanent one."

Jaegar glanced at Octavius, who knew his secret. He was turned back into a vampire by Octavius not because the Life's Blood did not work on him. Turned by his own choice so he could have the strength and speed to protect Kalina.

"Jaegar, maybe you would know how that reversal process worked since you've experienced it yourself?" Kalina implored him.

"It's different with me," Jaegar said. "I can't tell you now, but I will when I get a chance. Right now I think I see those rogue vampires."

"Not good," Octavius said, squaring his shoulders. "They've hidden amongst a mass of people. Innocent civilians could get hurt." He pointed to a busy market street filled with vendors and street merchants.

"Crap," Jaegar said. "They could be anyone."

Kalina grabbed her rubies-encrusted stakes and forged ahead towards the crowd. "They're no different than any of the vampires we've hunted and staked before. They're in their vampire forms."

"We can sense a vampire several miles away," Octavius said. "This should be no problem."

"If we can keep them alive, we should," Kalina said. "They're human still, and I want to ask them questions, observe them. I think they are only acting crazy when they turn back to vampires. But I wouldn't know unless I get a chance to study them."

Jaegar broke out into a grin. "I was gone only a few weeks and now you sound like your brother Justin."

"I've enrolled in college," Kalina said. "On the pre-med track. I think it's in my blood to become a doctor, Jaegar."

"Just like your brother," Octavius said, pulling Kalina to him in a hug. "Just like your scientist father and mother." He kissed the top of her head

74

affectionately. "Just like the good old doctor from China, your ancestor, who created and discovered Life's Blood. I am very proud of you, Kalina."

Jaegar took Kalina's hand and pulled her to him, surprising and angering Octavius a bit. "Speaking of the good old doctor whose legend we've been tossing all around...I've met him."

"What? How?" Kalina asked. "He was from Ancient China? Were you around then? Were you a vampire then? Did Octavius meet him, too? Octavius was a vampire far longer than you so he probably would have..."

"Unfortunately, I haven't," Octavius said.

"But how?"

"I traveled back in time," Jaegar said. "I'll explain later when we round up these rogues, but just know this, the good doctor and his daughter Shin Shin were truly remarkable. I see where you get that nobility and strength of character now."

Kalina blushed. "Jaegar, that's such a nice thing for you to say."

"Indeed," Octavius noted. "I'll go ahead first to round up the rogues. I could probably handle this myself if you two want to catch up, but the longer we stay here, the harder it is to catch them." He leaned in and whispered quietly into Kalina's ear. "I'll take care of Neriti too. Keep your guard up when she's near. She's been eavesdropping on us. Keep talking for another minute, then join me in the Marketplace...Jaegar too." Like a gust of wind, he was gone.

"So Jaegar, tell me more about the doctor and Shin Shin. Was it true about his experiments? How was it like being in that time period?"

Jaegar couldn't help smiling as he remembered his brief but memorable interaction with the doctor and Shin Shin. "He was tall and quite good-looking for a man, of course," Jaegar said. "But did you know he was a master swordsman, who once served as one of the guardians to the Empress?"

"So noble," Kalina said. "Handsome, too? I somehow didn't expect that. I thought he would be this white-haired bushy eyebrow old man with a long beard."

"I had pictured him that way too, until I met him," Jaegar said.

"How did you go back in time? Is this some kind of vampire power?" Kalina asked.

"More like fey magic, Kal," Jaegar said. "This ring," he lifted his right hand where he wore the ring on his index finger. "It looks like a diamond ring, but it is made of crystal...from the fey. It transported back into time, but not really because I wanted to, but because Neriti did, gluing herself to me so she could control the magic from this ring." Jaegar looked around. "Talking about the witch. Where is she? We can't lose sight of her."

"I know," Kalina said, looking around. Octavius had told her to keep talking, to cause a distraction.

"I could sense someone around," Jaegar said, taking out his stake.

"Jaegar, let's head over to the Marketplace. Octavius is there and..."

"Kalina," Jaegar stopped. "Your hand. That ring. Is that from Octavius?"

"This?" Kalina lifted her left hand, showing a diamond ring on her ring finger. She blushed. "No, not from Octavius. I wear it to remind myself of you,

Jaegar. I found it in your belongings at that hotel."

"The true Blood Ring," Jaegar muttered. "You had it all this time." He pulled her into his chest and kissed her softly. "It meant a lot to me when you said you wore it on your ring finger as a reminder of me." He kissed her more urgently now. "Does that mean you care for me?"

Kalina kissed him back, savoring his lips on hers like before. "Of course I do, Jaegar. You don't have to doubt that. My heart nearly broke when I thought you died."

"Kal," Jaegar wrapped his arms tighter around her. "I love you so much, I couldn't stop thinking about you."

"So that's what you've been doing!" Octavius' booming voice carried through to them from across the park. Behind him was a line of five vampire men, tied at the wrist by a rope. He led the men over to Kalina. "Caught the rogues. Now where's the other?"

"We lost her too," Kalina frowned.

"No frowning," Jaegar smiled at her. "We'll find her. But first, don't you want to question these rogues?"

"I will," Kalina walked confidently towards them. She stood in front of them, wielding her stake and slapping it against the palm of her other hand. "Now," she addressed them. "When did you changed into vampires? Was it some kind of extreme emotional state or..."

"Yes, miss," a blonde-haired man in his 30s said. "I changed into a vampire after 15 years as a human, right when my girl, a Carrier, told me she was leaving me for my best friend."

"I turned when I lost my job," another vampire said.

"Same here!" Another one said.

"I got sick," another one admitted.

"So it was due to some kind of event, something in your life that triggered it," Kalina said. "Have you turned before and was it because of something you felt?"

"Yes," one vampire said.

"A dozen times," another said.

"Okay," Kalina announced. "I think I got it. Now. We're going to keep you someplace safe where you can change back into humans. In this state, you are almost out of control, ruled by your emotions. Think of it as a state of mind. When you change back into humans, we will let you go."

"I'll take them," a familiar voice said.

Kalina turned around and saw a tall, handsome chestnut-haired young man with a kind face standing back a ways. Stuart.

Standing next to him was Justin and Kalina's Carrier mother, Max.

Chapter 7

"Jaegar's alive!" Justin rushed over to Jaegar and enveloped him in a brotherly bear hug. "How? Why? Not need to explain why now, we have some important things to take care of."

"Jaegar!" Stuart came up to him and wrapped his arm around Jaegar's shoulders, pulling him in close. "As much as I hate to admit it, I'm glad you're back."

"As much as I hate to admit it," Jaegar said to Stuart, "I'm happy to see that hideous face of yours, too." Jaegar grabbed Stuart's arm and twisted it playfully, intending to be the alpha brother with him as was his usual greeting to his little brother Stuart after some sort of long absence.

Stuart broke free of Jaegar's hold, and pinned him down to the ground, the way an alpha dog showed a lesser pup his power.

Jaegar's eyes narrowed slightly with

suspicion. Stuart had been turned by Kalina's Life's Blood which worked, transforming him into the human he had longed to become. One look into Stuart's eyes, and he could see Stuart had turned back into a vampire.

"Not fair, bro," Jaegar said, "You caught me by surprise." He jumped up from the ground using only his legs to hop up. He leaned in to whisper into Stuart's ear. "I know you're a vampire. Once again."

"That's one reason why I'm all the way here in China. Flew here, vampire-style," Stuart said.

"Stuart, Justin, and Mom!" Kalina cried. "Why are you all here?"

Max walked up to Kalina. "We have an emergency of our own. Go to Stuart. He'll explain." Max walked over to Jaegar, while Kalina went to Stuart. "Welcome back, Jaegar," Max said. "For a while there, we all thought we lost one of family members."

"Family?" Jaegar asked.

"Of course, you're one of ours," Max said. "You are an important part of our family, don't you know?"

Jaegar looked down at his feet then looked

earnestly at Max...Max who looked like an older version of Kalina. "Coming from you, that means a lot. Thank you."

"So," Max said. "You were turned from vampire to human to vampire again. How do you think we can solve this situation with the Life's Blood vampires turning back into vampires but a crazed version of themselves? You turned back to a vampire, but you're the same. How did you stay sane?"

Jaegar pulled Max aside. "Promise you won't tell Kal this. I will eventually tell her in my own time and in my own way, but I want to be the one telling her. It's different with me. Life's Blood did turn me human. Kalina's blood made me mortal again. She loved me enough to give me that gift of life. But because I felt too weak and helpless as a human while vampires attacked Kalina and I couldn't protect her, I asked Octavius to turn me back into a vampire. His way was permanent."

Max's eyebrow cocked slightly up, the only indication of a reaction from her. "You returned back to a vampire to protect Kalina?"

"I am a knight through and through, Max.

83

Blood Ring (Pulse #9)

Back when I first lived as a human in the Medieval Ages, even as a vampire. Kalina is my lady, and I will protect her forever, even if she ends up loving another more than I."

Max put her hand on Jaegar's shoulder. "Oh I think she has pretty strong feelings for you, Jaegar. You can't doubt that. She was heartbroken when she thought you had died. Even Octavius couldn't cheer her up."

Jaegar froze for a second. His heart began racing. While Octavius was there with her, Kalina was thinking of him, Jaegar. His heart soared with love for Kalina at the realization that Kalina truly did love him.

As if she could read his mind, Max said, "You came back to us for a reason. Now find that purpose."

"Kal, Justin, Octavius, Max, and Stuart," Jaegar called. "Come here."

Everyone came over except Stuart, who remain guarding the rogue vampires.

"What is it?" Kalina asked.

"The good doctor's house. I visited it at the

time he was alive. I think I can find his works, his records on Life's Blood. Maybe we can fix this without more bloodshed."

"His house? Where is it?" Justin asked. "It may work. With my medical training as a blood specialist, I may be able to figure out why the Life's Blood Vampires are shifting back and forth between crazed vampire and human."

"Take us there, Jaegar," Octavius said in his general voice, placing a hand on his shoulder.

"Can everyone use flight?" Jaegar asked.

Stuart walked up to Jaegar. "I heard the tail end of your conversation." He smiled widely. "In a way, I missed being a vampire with enhanced senses, strength, and flying abilities."

"Where are the rogue vampires?" Justin asked. "I'll run tests on them later when I can try out the new formula to Life's Blood once we find the doctor's journals, but in the meantime, I can't help being curious as to the place, the house Life's Blood was discovered."

"Like I said," Stuart laughed, "I missed being a vampire...of course not the craving of blood part but, many other things, like this." He gestured towards a luxury hotel hi-rise. "I marched the vampires over to that hotel, compelled the desk clerk to check them into two adjacent rooms, and compelled the security guard to watch them."

"I take it, you're coming with us," Jaegar said.

"Of course I am," Stuart said. "I'm one of the affected ones. You need me to test things out. Besides, Jaegar, I need to ask you a favor."

Jaegar saw the seriousness in Stuart's eyes and nodded.

"I can't tell you now, but later," Stuart said. "You're my brother. I can trust you to grant my favor."

"Alright, tell me later, but now, we have some flying to do!" Jaegar said. "Everyone, follow me. We're heading north of here to the top of the mountain ranges. It's a village known as Heaven's Mountain. It's an abandoned village now, but back then, it was a thriving village." He looked at Kalina. "Do you want to ride on my back?"

"Jaegar?" Kalina laughed. "I haven't ride on anyone's back for a good while now. I haven't needed to since I gained that vampire ability. But…"

"I'm not asking you because you need to," Jaegar said. "But because you want to. And," he gazed deeply into her chocolate eyes. "I want you to."

"Alright," she said, standing behind him and plopping her arms around his neck. She leaned in close to whisper into his ears. "If it means I can hold onto you, I will."

Jaegar took off, followed by Octavius, Stuart, Justin, and Max. Soon, they were flying above the clouds where no human eye could see them, and heading quickly through the different provinces of China.

"Kal, are you comfortable?" Jaegar asked when they were flying slightly ahead of everyone.

She nestled against his neck. "I am, Jaegar," she said. "I missed this."

"I missed you," Jaegar said with such longing in his voice. "I miss you so much I thought I'd die being apart from you."

Kalina tighten her hold on his neck with her right arm, but used her left arm to run her fingers down his chest and to his waist.

Blood Ring (Pulse #9)

Jaegar sucked in a deep breath as waves of arousal ran through him. "Kal, you're making me want you right here, right now," he growled. "God how much I want you."

Kal whispered into his ear, "You know what, Jaegar? I'm supposed to act all shy and innocent because I'm a young woman and a virgin, but the truth is, I want you too. Badly."

Jaegar gulped. "Kalina, don't say things you don't mean, please. It'll only get my hopes too high."

"I mean it, Jaegar," Kalina said. "When I thought you were dead, and I found this ring...the Blood Ring, I thought it was an engagement ring, and for a sudden moment, I could imagine us together, as man and woman, with a future, and I thought, 'If Jaegar was still alive and had presented me with this ring, I would have said yes.' The thought made me so happy, that for a while, I forgot you weren't alive any longer. Now that, Jaegar would be my biggest regret...not telling you how much I love you. So much that..."

A small plane flew by beneath them, drowning out Kalina's voice. Jaegar thought she was too shy about her feelings to say them out loud to him. Maybe she will another time, he thought. It didn't matter now. Their brief moment of privacy was over. Octavius, Max, Stuart, and Justin were flying shoulder to shoulder with Jaegar now, heading down into the green leafy terrain below, yet still high up in the mountains.

Jaegar dropped down first onto a treetop and helped Kalina off his back. Then he descended from the tree with Kalina close behind. Together they walked through the small patch of forest leading to the village and into the village gates.

Jaegar remembered the village was devastated, abandoned, and forgotten for hundreds of years when he was last here with Kalina and the others. Now...

Spread out before him, was an idyllic charming and well-preserved village, filled with people walking the concrete sidewalk, tourists shopping, and shops of every kind which filled the main street, offering everything a local and visitor could want.

"I don't understand," Jaegar said. "This village

was like a ghost town. We fought Mal here and Balthazar."

"I remembered," Kalina said. "It was a ghost town, but now...it's as though it's thriving...a charming village steep in history yet still in pace with modern times."

"This is the village we fought Mal and Molotov?" Octavius walked up to them.

"Impossible!" Max said, walking with Justin to join them.

"I kinda like it here," Justin said looking around. "I mean, I would visit and stay here a bit." His eyes brighten with excitement. "I don't know how this could be the same village we had our battle but some kind of magic must be at work because my logical scientist mind says this is impossible!"

Stuart strode in last, casually, yet good-naturedly. "I'm due for a vacation. This off-the-beaten-path village complete with history, natural beauty, modern conveniences, and luxury inns with hot springs, is exactly what I need."

"Another time," Octavius said. "We need to find the doctor's house and his records."

90

"Follow me!" Jaegar said. "I remember this place like it was yesterday...literally." He walked down the street with everyone in tow, blending into the village like other tourists and locals. He let his feet guide him, and found himself standing in front of the doctor's estate, perfectly preserved as he had remembered when the doctor lived here. "It was just like yesterday," Jaegar said. "Everything's here."

He walked up to the sweet old lady with a kind smile and laughing eyes. "Can we go inside?"

She held out her hand.

"Oh, money?" Jaegar looked around. He didn't have any local currency.

Stuart walked over and handed the lady some bills. "I've got it. Got some local currency when I was depositing the rogue vampires at the hotel." He smirked, clearly enjoying himself as a vampire again.

The old lady gave Stuart tickets for everyone in their party and pointed to a room at the far end of the courtyard. They made their way through the courtyard to the main room. A young woman was there to collect their tickets and provide them with a hot cup of tea.

Blood Ring (Pulse #9)

"Delicious," Octavius said, thanking the woman.

"Hit the spot," Justin said.

"Smooth as silk," Stuart said.

"Robust and flavorful," Jaegar said.

Kalina and Max looked at each other with amusement. Then they drank their tea.

"Aromatic," Max said.

Kalina didn't say anything but smiled. She couldn't say anything. To her, the tea was the taste of blood.

She looked down. It almost looked like blood, but when she blinked again, it was a clear amber hue. "What is this?" she asked the woman.

"Whatever nourishes you," the woman said. "The Tea of Dreams."

"Oh," Kalina said.

"This way," the young woman said, after she collected their teacups on a tray and placed it on a nearby table.

They followed her down the hall and into a large living room, filled with vases, golden carvings of phoenixes, foxes, and dragons. "Sit," she said, gesturing at the wooden ornate chairs lined up next to each other in the center of the room, along the main path of the living room. "You all came here for a purpose, a need. I read your dreams."

"How?" Jaegar asked.

"From the tea," the woman said. "Don't worry. I am a friend. I am one of the last remaining ones from Shin Shin, the doctor's daughter's line.

"You're a Carrier?" Kalina asked.

The young woman shook her head, sending her long black hair flying around her face.

Beautiful and exquisite, Justin thought. Could she be another relative to Kalina and Max?

"No, I was never bestowed that gift or curse," she said. "But rather, I was given the gift of sight. My name is Grace. Dr. Shaw was my ancestor." She looked at Max and Kalina. "As he was to you. You are welcome here."

"We don't have much time to visit," Jaegar said. "We need to find Dr. Shaw's records so we can help with a new condition the turned vampires are now facing."

"I shall bring you what you need," Grace said.

Blood Ring (Pulse #9)

She walked back behind a wall and came out shortly with some helpers in tow, carrying a large wooden and ancient teakwood chest with intricate carvings. They placed the chest in front of Jaegar. "The doctor's records," she said. "It's sealed, been sealed for hundreds of years. No one has ever opened it, although many have tried. Many believed it was sealed by magic, and only the one it was intended for could open it."

Grace turned to Stuart, Octavius, Max, and Justin. "I shall come back with what you came here for."

They all looked at each other with amazement. Didn't they all came for the same reason?

Grace walked behind the wall and returned a few minutes later with the helpers behind her, carrying objects on a tray.

A tray with a small piece of bamboo stalk was placed in front of Stuart. He looked up, confused.

A tray with a child's wooden top was placed in front of Max.

Then a tray with a glass vial was placed in front of Justin.

A tray with a piece of paper was placed in front of Octavius.

Finally, a tray with a golden key was placed in front of Kalina.

"These are your most inner dreams and purposes combined," Grace said. "Now I will leave you to yourself. You are free to stay here throughout the night and however long you need to accomplish what you came here for. We will close the estate to tourists for now."

"Thank you," Kalina said to Grace, walking up to her. "I wished I knew of you sooner."

"What is important is that you are all here now, as the doctor wished."

"All this," Kalina gestured widely. "How is this possible? I thought everything in this village...how could this village survive the pillaging and attacks all these years and remain as it was. This house, the doctor's things?"

"Legend said," Grace began, "that the doctor once fought a black dragon with a knight from another realm. The knight prophesied that the doctor will one day create a cure to help humans and vampires exist together, that he must preserve his home and village since it will be a thriving place one day where tourists can learn of the doctor's plight and legend."

Jaegar closed his eyes. His visit back in time changed things...this village, the doctor, and most likely the doctor's formula for Life's Blood.

"How?" Jaegar said to himself. "Besides the fact, Life's Blood vampires turned humans could revert back to being vampires, what else was different, and now, was he the only one who would remember?

"Open!" Jaegar said to the chest. Surely he was the one the doctor had intended to open the chest after all these years.

The chest did not move.

Jaegar pounded the lock, but it remained closed, impenetrable.

Jaegar used his ring and pointed it to the chest, "I command you to open!"

The chest remained closed.

"I don't get it," Jaegar said flexing his shoulders and arms. "Guess I have to break it open."

"Hold on," Kalina walked past him and inserted the key from the tray into the lock, twisted it, and watched the top swing up on its own.

"Kalina was the one the doctor had intended to find this chest, but how did he know?" Max said.

"I told him about Kalina," Jaegar said. It made sense now.

"Great," Justin said. "Now the chest is open so we're looking for records..." he walked over to the chest and began carefully taking papers, books, scrolls, and wooden boxes out. "There is so much stuff in here, Kal!" Justin said. "Come over and help."

Kalina began sorting through the papers, while Justin carefully removed objects from within the chest, lining them up neatly on a large wooden table behind them.

Jaegar stepped in to help, somehow being able to read the materials in ancient Chinese.

"Here's his journal!" Jaegar said, holding up a leather bound book the size of a family photo album.

"There's more!" Justin said, lifting ten volumes out of the chest. He laid them down on the table and flipped through one. "Dr. Shaw kept

97

meticulous notes. He is a Godsend! And...how am able to read ancient Chinese?"

Justin sat down and pored over the books. Kalina sat down next to him. "Somehow I could too," she said. "Everyone...Stuart, Octavius, Mom! Could you take one volume each and go through it? It'll be faster, and somehow something tells me, we can all have the ability to read these records."

"Sure," Stuart said, grabbing two volumes and propping down at the table to speed read through them. "Done," he said minutes later.

"Show off!" Jaegar said.

"Being a vampire has its advantages!" Stuart said, crossing his arms.

"Then read the one I'm reading," Jaegar said.

Stuart walked over, opened the books, and quickly flipped through the pages in record speed. "Done."

"Here are my notes," Max said, putting it down on top of the table."

"Here are mine," Octavius said.

"This volume tells about the history of Life's Blood's ingredients," Justin said. "It's almost like reading folklore and mythology. Fascinating."

"This one," Kalina got up and stretched. "Tells how the doctor was able to finally improve the Life's Blood through testing hundreds of subjects, to the point he was able to mitigate the side effects of having a vampire who forcefully drank blood from a Carrier become a crazed, invincible, and evil immortal vampire. Rather, those vampires will remain unaffected. No invincible or immortal powers. They could however become crazed and hot-headed, ruled by their animalistic natures.

"Really?" Jaegar asked. "So the Mals and the Molotovs would never have happened."

"What about the fate of vampires whom the Carrier gave their blood freely?" Octavius asked. "Nothing in my volume said anything about the Life's Blood, but how the doctor believed vampires originated as abominations of the fey, especially the one Pixie Queen Neranda. Sounds like Neriti. He even described her personality and ruthlessness precisely."

"The doctor wrote that a Carrier's blood can be used to cleanse the guilt of a vampire, by turning him human. Through love, the Carrier's blood can help a vampire start anew. And," Kalina read, "Carriers do not need to remain chaste to bestow this gift to the vampire she loved."

Kalina glanced at Octavius and met his eyes. She blushed before glancing over at Jaegar. Jaegar's heated gaze nearly took her breath away.

She cleared her throat. "Carriers are not bound to one vampire. Life's Blood is a cure for these vampires. Keeping it scarce and just for a chosen few will cause pain and suffering to the ones not chosen. Therefore, a Carrier's Life Blood can be given freely to those she loved without a need for an exclusive romantic love. A Life's Blood Carrier can and should love and turn as many vampires they can, to spread the cure and save both humans and vampire kind."

"Wow," Jaegar said. "That means, all of us, whom Kalina loves could be turned into humans without having a romantic attachment. Even Justin."

"Yes," Kalina said. "I would love that, and it would be my desire to help all of you become human again. But...we still don't know about the reversal process. Did anyone read anything about that?"

Stuart spoke up. "Volume 7 said the doctor's subjects had turned human, but a few would appear as vampires once again. He suspected they were turned by vampires, but eventually he concluded it must be from the unknown ingredient, the wildcard he used to create the essence of Life's Blood itself."

"Didn't he used the blood of the strongest vampire to get the strength and immortality for Life's Blood?" Kalina asked Octavius.

"Yes, but not by choice. He was glamored into it, which can explain why he didn't take notes on it," Octavius said. "Who else could that be...the strongest, most invincible vampire that ever walked the Earth? Neriti."

"Nereti!" Everyone said.

"The wildcard ingredient. With her blood entrenched into Life's Blood, there is no telling what side effects could come up," Octavius said.

"Precisely," Kalina said. "But that won't stop me from turning vampires to humans. The rewards of that is worth it, isn't it?"

Stuart nodded "yes", while Jaegar, Justin, and

Octavius looked at each other. Kalina was looking at them, too, as though she was offering her blood for them.

"I like being immortal, sis," Justin said. "I want to use my vampire abilities to keep doing research on Life's Blood, but...I don't want to keep drinking people's blood and the way I have to do it to keep alive."

Kalina threw a stick at Justin. "Don't worry, I'm not turning you now. Just a thought, though."

"Now about those rogue vampires...what do we do about them?" Max asked.

Kalina threw up her hands in bewilderment. "Nothing in these books about that. But maybe we just have to get a sample of Neriti's blood to experiment on, so we can know it's effects."

"Great idea!" Justin chimed in. "She's the necessary ingredient after all."

"Question is," Kalina asked. "Where is she, and what is she up to?"

Chapter 8

The gang decided to break for the night, going out to explore the village for dinner and a little shopping.

They went to a noodle house where Max and Kalina ate bowls and bowls of noodles of all type. "Eat up!" Max shoved one bowl after another towards Kalina. "You need your strength."

"I'm eating as much as I can," Kalina said with her mouth full. "This isn't an all-you-can-eat buffet, you know."

"It's delicious, that's what it is," Max said, gulping down another bowl of noodles. After her fifth bowl, she got up and excused herself. "I'm going to find the restroom."

The vampires Jaegar, Octavius, Justin, and Stuart looked around, pretending to eat their bowls of noodles with relish. Instead, they were all too aware of the hot warm blood flowing through the veins of the noodle house's patrons.

Blood Ring (Pulse #9)

Justin slammed down his teacup. "This tea is good, but I am going to faint if I don't get any food."

"Be discreet," Octavius said.

"I'm starving, myself," Jaegar said.

"Where is vampire wine when you need it?" Stuart asked. "Note to myself, continue the manufacturing and distributing of vampire wine everywhere, especially to China." Stuart got up. "I'm going to find some red wine. It's something to sustain my appetite, but after being human for a while, taking blood from another human just isn't very appealing to me."

Justin stood up and left the table, going outside.

"I'm sorry," Octavius said to Kalina, kissing her cheeks. "I must eat or I can't fight." He got up and left the restaurant.

"What about you?" Kalina asked Jaegar.

"I'm staying right here," he said. "Even the thought of taking someone's blood unwillingly is becoming distasteful to me."

"Oh?" Kalina asked. "You used to boast that you will take what you want whenever you wanted.

What happened?"

Jaegar fixed his eyes on her eyes and moved down to her full lips. "To tell you the truth, Kalina...*you* happened."

He kissed Kalina softly for a long time while slipping his fingers through hers. They kept kissing for a while, sitting in the middle of the noodle house, while everyone stopped eating and started watching them.

"Hey, stop pushing me," Stuart's voice exploded from the back of the room, at the doorway of the kitchen. "I just want some more red wine. Vampire wine, if you have any." He slurred his words and stumbled out.

A waiter carrying a tray of food walked past him and he stumbled over him, sending the food flying all over a table of rough-looking men and splattering their suits. "I don't feel too well," Stuart said before barfing over one of them.

The man stood up, a look of disgust and anger making his face look almost cartoonish red.

"Hey, I'm sorry," Stuart said. "I'll clean it up." He began wiping the man's shirt with the man's tie.

Blood Ring (Pulse #9)

"I hope it doesn't stain, but red wine on white is killer to get out."

"Stop touching me, you Ass!" the man bellowed. He looked over at his friends at the table. "Get this ass to take his hands off me!"

A burly muscle-bound stocky man with a crew cut walked over to Stuart and grabbed his shirt, getting ready to punch him.

"Whoa whoa!" Justin appeared out of nowhere to stand between burly man and Stuart. "He's drunk. Look at him. He didn't mean to touch the guy. Give him a break."

The burly man sat down while Justin took Stuart and attempted to walk him past the table.

Stuart let Justin guide him past the table, but when they attempted to walk past the next table where a lovely young woman wearing a plunging shirt was seated next to her boyfriend, Stuart lunged at her neck, pinning her down on the table, with dishes of food flying everywhere.

Her boyfriend punched Stuart, while Justin tried to ply him off the woman. It was as if Stuart had lost complete control.

106

Jaegar stood up and tried to get the boyfriend off Stuart while Octavius rushed in to grab Stuart and wrenched him from the frightened and screaming woman.

All around them, people had gotten out of their chairs, running.

"Monster! Ghosts!" they shouted.

"He had demon eyes," someone cried.

The cook came out of the kitchen with a cleaver and took swings at Stuart, but struck Octavius in the shoulder. Octavius bellowed in pain as blood poured from his open wound.

Max grabbed Octavius before the cook could take another swing. She kicked the cook in the face, and shoved Octavius over to Kalina. "Take care of him. He's got an artery cut. He's bleeding too much." Max gave the cook another kick to disable him, sending the cleaver flying into the wall. "Your food isn't that great anyways," she said. "Made me sick to my stomach, and Stuart is ill too."

Kalina rushed out of the noodle house, with Octavius leaning on her. She bumped into a young woman with straight black hair, carrying some candles and incense sticks. Grace.

"Quick," Grace said. "Take Octavius to the doctor's house. I've sealed it from outsiders. You can treat him there. In the meantime, I'm going to burn these incense sticks and candles."

"What are they?" Kalina asked.

"Compulsion candles," Grace said. "You know how vampires can compel people to forget things? The doctor figured out a way to recreate this. He kept these ancient candles hidden in a vault. So there are some things we humans could do even without vampire powers," she smiled. She placed the candles around the restaurant and lit them. "Soon everyone here will forget there were vampires dining amongst you or on you. Soon everyone will forget tonight's incidence inside the noodle house when it involves vampires."

Octavius groaned and Kalina waved bye to Grace, hurrying over to the doctor's house.

Chapter 9

Kalina was exhausted, carrying Octavius all the way to the doctor's house and laying him down on a bed in one of the rooms. Octavius lost so much blood, he was almost deadweight leaning on Kalina. Kalina had to do something. Without blood, Octavius could not heal.

Yet there was no human blood around to give Octavius. Except...her own.

She bit into her wrist and lifted Octavius' head, offering her blood to him. With his eyes closed, he latched onto her wrists before pushing her away when he realized it was Kalina's blood he was drinking. "No, I can't, Kalina. I can't risk turning. Not when there is a possibility I can become a crazed vampire."

"You need blood, Octavius," she said, offering him her wrist. "Please Octavius. I've always wanted to offer you my blood, but you kept rejecting me. Is it because you don't love me? You don't want to become human to be with me?"

Octavius grabbed Kalina's hair to pull her to his face. "How could you say I don't love you?" he asked miserably. "I love you so much I can't become human for you. I'll become useless to you as a human. I can't face not being able to protect you if I do."

"Octavius," Kalina said, kissing him. "I'll love you no matter what, vampire or human. But I want you to live." She raised her wrist and filled her mouth with her blood.

With her other hand, she ran her fingers up and down his inner thighs, making him moan. Her hand brushed the bulging front part of his pants and he let out a "Ahh woman, you drive me crazy with desire for you."

She kissed him then, dripping her blood into his mouth, feeding him with her mouth. "Accept your fate, General," Kalina said when her mouth was emptied of her blood. "When you met me, and had fallen for me, you knew you would eventually be turned by me."

110

Octavius' eyes blazed with hot desire and hunger. "I can't fight this, Kalina. You are my weakness, after all." He threw his head back and his fangs protruded. "I've been dreaming for ages, for this moment, Kalina." He licked her milky white neck and sank his teeth into her neck, groaning loudly as he drank from her. "Ah Kalina. You taste far better than any blood I've ever had. You are worth waiting for, my sweet beloved girl."

"Octavius," Kalina closed her eyes, wracked by the waves of pleasure flowing through her as Octavius drank from her.

After a while, he stopped and lifted his head. "Kalina, are you alright? Kalina?"

She opened her eyes and smiled weakly at him. "I'm fine, just need a little rest."

"I drank too much, I couldn't help myself," Octavius said. "I'm sorry."

"That's alright, you needed my blood," Kalina said. "Now rest." When Octavius closed his eyes, Kalina kissed his lips and said, "My dear Octavius. I will always love you, and I am glad you will finally experience being a human once again. Yet I am also glad for the doctor's glitch in Life's Blood. You can still shift into a vampire when you need to. You can have the best of both worlds along with the bad, but hopefully more good than bad."

She kissed him again before getting up and walking out of the room. She had finally given Octavius her blood and felt such pleasure of him drinking from her...all that she had imagined. Like Octavius, his kiss was so perfect, so wonderful...it would be difficult giving that up so she can finally be with the one she could never give up.

Chapter 10

Kalina ran back to the noodle house, looking for everyone. Where was Max? Where was Stuart and Justin? And, where was Jaegar?

The noodle house was now quiet and surprisingly sedate. The smell of spicy vanilla, cinnamon and other spices filled the air from the candles surrounding the restaurant.

The lights were still on, and people were once again eating at the tables.

Once again, the noodle house was at peace. Except at the back of the restaurant where there was a table outside near the back entrance of the building.

The Greystone Brothers were sitting at the picnic-style table on the same bench facing out. Stuart had his head on Jaegar's shoulder, while Max and Justin stood back, a little ways behind, leaning along a wall. The cook was with them, and Max was saying something to him, while applying ice to his face.

"You promise," Stuart said sadly. "If I get out-of-control as a vampire when I shift and I end up hurting the people I love, especially Kalina and Maeve; stake me." He took out the piece of bamboo from his pocket. "Use this bamboo and stake me."

"You're ridiculous," Jaegar said.

"I think this bamboo does represent me well. It is strong, but flexible. Able to stand alone, yet with a group. I think I like that Life's Blood does allow me to shift back and forth as a human and a vampire. As a human, I found I missed some things about being a vampire. Yet, as a vampire, I always thought being human was where it's at. For me, being both is an incredible and unbelievable dream. You did good, Jaegar, when you went back in time to meet the doctor. You changed the future and made it better."

"It was all the doctor's doing," Jaegar said. "He figured out that his experiments with Life's Blood as it was going was not the best way. Then he made adjustments. He figured out I was a vampire who loved a Carrier, yet wasn't the chosen love, so he made adjustments. And he knew he had to do

114

whatever it took to protect the ones he loved and the place that he loved, so he made adjustments as mayor of this village so that it would continue to thrive over the years."

"I'm so proud of you, Jaegar," Kalina said, startling Jaegar and Stuart from their talk.

Jaegar nearly dropped Stuart's head from his shoulder. "Kalina, thank God you're safe. That was fast thinking of Grace to compel everyone, wasn't it?"

"Yes," Kalina smiled. "I would love to get to know Grace better, and this village someday. But now...I'd like to talk to you."

Stuart chuckled. "Jaegar's in trouble, isn't he?"

"That depends," Kalina said. "Whether he's been good or bad."

Jaegar got up, eager to go anywhere with Kalina. "Sorry, Stuart, as much as I enjoyed our brotherly talk, nothing can compared to the sexy way Kalina just said, 'that depends'." He rushed over to Kalina and swooped her feet off the floor to hold her in his arms. "Where to? I'll take you."

"How about a treetop over there?" Kalina said,

pointing at one that just happened to be the same treetop Jaegar landed in when he fell out of the sky with Neriti the dragon.

"Alright," Jaegar said. "Anything you wish." He lifted into the air and held Kalina tightly while he landed on top of the trees and placed Kalina's arms around his neck. "We're here, on top of the mountains, on top of the world. What did you want to talk to me about?"

Kalina looked up into his brilliant beautiful blue eyes and sighed. "I'm so lucky," she said. "I have the love of the most amazing vampires and humans around. I don't want anything to change, yet I know I have to, for your sake and everyone else's."

Jaegar's smile disappeared and he looked serious. "Is something wrong? Kalina you can tell me anything."

"Yes," Kalina said, "Something is wrong. I can't move on unless you know this."

Jaegar suck in a deep breath and said, "What is it?" He was preparing to hear her say good-bye to him, to declare her love for someone else...a love far more deeper than the one she had for him...

116

"You're the one I want, Jaegar," Kalina said. "I finally realized it. I was immature and inexperienced with the feelings of romantic love before not knowing which way to go. I didn't want to hurt anyone's feelings nor lead anyone on. I love so many people. I love people. I wish the best for everyone, yet...when it comes to who I can't face not seeing everyday...I realized it was you. I love you, Jaegar. So much I want to give you my blood and everything else you crave."

Jaegar gazed deeply into her eyes, his lips curled up into a smile. "It's about time you came to your senses, crazy girl." He kissed her deeply then and said, "I'll take you, your gift, and everything else; and I don't intend to ever let go."

Epilogue

She finally had the Blood Ring in her hands. The one and only Blood Ring that would get her through the Wall of Ice. While they were all distracted with their care and love for each other, while that fool Jaegar and that usurper Kalina was declaring their love for each other, Neriti found the perfect opportunity to snatch the ring from Kalina's pocket. Now she was a few feet away from the Wall of Ice, and the Wolf Fey Prince was nowhere to be seen.

If this is the authentic ring, she could tear down this wall of ice, create a ring through the wall that would open the portal for her vampire minions to go in and out as they wish...to follow her into Feyland where she can set her army against the Winter and Summer Kingdoms. Now that they had a half human, half fey Empress of Feyland, she also knew they have the weaknesses of humankind too.

She looked all around her. Could the Wolf

118

Prince really be that easy to fool? Jaegar, she could understand...how she went along with his wishes with that of his, letting him believe it was truly his powers that caused her to shift. The truth was, it was her powers combined with his and the ring that created the magic.

With the ring on her right hand index finger, she pressed her palm along the smooth cold surface of the wall. She could feel the magic of the Frost flow through her. This wall, erected with the magic of both the Summer and the Winter Kingdoms of Feyland was filled with enchantment....

She raised her hand up high and struck down onto the wall in front of her. The ring on her finger sparked and steamed with red fire. It was the fire from the Blood Ring.

"Ahhhh!" Neriti clenched her teeth in pain as the scorching red flames burned through her. She must resist this pain. She pushed on, using the flames to heat the wall. She pushed on, for what seemed like hours with this red flame burning through her like a torch until at last, there was a crack. She pushed on further until the crack widen and lengthen.

"Just a little bit more," Neriti said to herself.

*****

Somewhere at the opposite ends of Feyland in the Grand Hall of the Winter Court, Empress Breena looked up from where she was examining an ancient scroll that the Pixie King Delano had left for her...a scroll that laid claim to all the territories of the north and east...the Winter lands and Autumn Springs. Even those of Summer.

Although the Seasonal Fey were on friendly and peaceful terms with the Pixie Kingdom, lately there had been some unrest amongst the Pixies.

"So Delano wants to laid claim by Ancient Law to these lands? But that's almost all of Feyland!" Breena exclaimed to King Kian and her Head of Security, Logan the Wolf Prince. "If he doesn't get those lands, does he want to start a war?"

"But all of Feyland is now united; the Winter and the Summer Kingdoms are at last together. The Wolf Fey and woodlands animals – minotaurs, sartres, all," King Kian said. "We should be able to put down an uprising should it begin with all of our forces."

"We should," Logan spoke up, "but there is a problem brewing across the Land Beyond the Crystal River...one we didn't factored into the equation. We wanted to protect the humans from our rogue fey, especially the Wolf Fey, with their newfound fey magic, but we haven't anticipated the rogues already residing in the Land Beyond the Crystal River...the Dark Fey. Vampires."

"What?" Breena exclaimed in disbelief. "Vampires? They're fey, too?"

Logan almost laughed at Breena's shocked expression.

"Are there really vampires?" she asked Logan. "I thought it was all folklore, romance novels, and sparkly films."

"Well, since there are werewolves or wolf shifters, what do you think?" Logan grinned.

"If you didn't just say that, Logan, you being you, I would've chucked this scroll at you."

Blood Ring (Pulse #9)

"I had to fight one off at the Wall of Ice," Logan said. "There was another one, a turned vampire from human. He was alright so I don't think all vampires are bad. But the woman...she was once fey, banished by the ancient ones for violating some of the most sacred fey laws, including the mass kidnapping and murder of countless humans..."

"The once great Pixie Queen Neranda?" Kian asked.

"Who?" Breena asked.

"She was Delano's wife, a pure Pixie, who couldn't bear him children but there was no love lost between them. It was more a political marriage than for love. She was also known for her cruelty and experiments with the blood of young fey women to obtain their beauty," Kian said. He looked at Logan. "So she wants to get back into Feyland after all this time. I could only wonder why."

"The timing with Delano and the Pixies' declaration can't be mere coincidence," Breena said.

"I agree," Kian said.

"She is the Vampire Queen, with an army of blood-thirsty vampires she commands with absolute control. If she crosses over along with her vampire herd, unite with the Pixies, and awaken the Dark Hordes like Delano did last time," Logan paused. "Well, many fey will be slaughtered. If the Vampire Queen is restored to full power along with the strength of the vampires, not only will she try to destroy Feyland and all whom she felt have wronged her in Feyland, but she has her eyes set on ruling all and destroying all in the Land Beyond the Crystal River."

Breena looked over at Kian.

So we are looking at the possibility of a war between worlds.

Not if we can prevent it, my love.

Logan could tell Breena and Kian were communicating telepathically. It was the betrothed fey connection they've shared since childhood. As much as he could be happy for Breena and Kian, still a part of him felt a tinged of jealousy. He couldn't remember all the details, but he once was very close to Breena. Might have even been deeply in love with her. Logan shook his head. He needed to concentrate, get his head wrapped around this potentially devastating situation.

"We need to secure the Wall from invaders like Neriti. We must add more sentries at the Wall from now on. I will recruit more knights and some of the wolf fey," Logan said. "The other vampires there like the one named Jaegar, seem to want to protect the humans from Neriti and her army. They fought against her for ages. If Neriti truly is this powerful, which I believe she is, then we need all the help we can get. I will go find Jaegar and the other vampires as soon as I get the new recruits and..."

CRAAACK!!!

From a far distance, the sound of shattered ice echoed throughout the land.

Breena, Kian, and Logan looked at each other in shock.

"I thought magic could repel her from the Wall," Logan said. "But I see we need more than that."

"Whatever it is," Breena said, walking up to the large window overlooking the Kingdom of Winter and of Summer. "We will fight her...this Neriti...with everything we've got."

*****

The PULSE family will continue in the spin-off, which also features characters from the Bitter Frost Series:

Beyond The Crystal River

Ring of Ice (Frost Worlds: Beyond the Crystal River #1)
- Just Released at: amzn.com/B00U4KUO5W

*****

Get all the books in the PULSE Vampires Series – Now Complete and Available!

PULSE
https://www.amazon.com/PULSE-Vampire-Book-1-ebook/dp/B0041D8CPC

Life's Blood (PULSE Vampires #2)
https://www.amazon.com/gp/product/B0046LV9VI

Blood Burned (PULSE Vampires #3)
https://www.amazon.com/gp/product/B004BA52F8

Blood Ring (Pulse #9)

Blue Blood (PULSE Vampires #4)
https://www.amazon.com/gp/product/B004NSV5KY

Blood Bond (PULSE Vampires #5)
https://www.amazon.com/gp/product/B004NSV5KY

Blood Legacy (PULSE Vampires #6)
https://www.amazon.com/gp/product/B006G2EC4G

Blood Rights (PULSE Vampires #7)
https://www.amazon.com/Blood-Rights-PULSE-Vampire-7-ebook/dp/B008CGX2JK

Blood Curse (PULSE Vampires #8)
https://www.amazon.com/gp/product/B00IQQ3IUO

Blood Ring (PULSE Vampires #9)
https://www.amazon.com/Blood-Ring-PULSE-Vampire-9-ebook/dp/B00OYMXNCM

Ring of Ice (Beyond Crystal River – Bitter Frost and PULSE Converge)
https://www.amazon.com/Ring-Ice-Frost-Worlds-Trilogy-ebook/dp/B00U4KUO5W

The FROST SERIES – Now Complete!

Kailin Gow

Bitter Frost
http://www.amazon.com/Bitter-Frost-Wolf-Books-ebook/dp/B0041HXP2S

Forever Frost
https://www.amazon.com/Forever-Frost-Bitter-TM-ebook/dp/B0041HXNUW

Silver Frost
http://www.amazon.com/Silver-Frost-Bitter-Series-ebook/dp/B004GHNDXO/

Frost Kisses
http://www.amazon.com/Frost-Kisses-Bitter-Series-ebook/dp/B004S311FI/

Midnight Frost
http://www.amazon.com/Midnight-Frost-Bitter-Series-ebook/dp/B005O1AIB6/

Frost Fire
http://www.amazon.com/Frost-Fire-Series-ebook/dp/B006LY3B32/

Spring Frost
http://www.amazon.com/Spring-Series-Fantasy-Adventure-ebook/dp/B007SMH2T0/

Enchanted Frost
https://www.amazon.com/Enchanted-Frost-Romantic-Fantasy-Adventure-ebook/dp/B00ADF96DE

Blood Ring (Pulse #9)

The Fairy Letters
http://www.amazon.com/The-Fairy-Letters-Series-ebook/dp/B0057YXIA8/

Watch the spin-off Super Supers TV Series, featuring Bitter Frost characters:

Super Supers – No Fan of the Ban:

https://www.amazon.com/Super-Supers-No-Fan-Ban/dp/B01MS72YSF

Super Supers – Fight for Feyland

https://www.amazon.com/Super-Supers-Bitter-Feyland-Breenas/dp/B06XDHV1ZN

Super Supers - PULSE Vampires Vs. Zombies

https://www.amazon.com/Super-Supers-Vampires-Zombies-Kalinas/dp/B06XP48QFH

Kailin Gow

GET IN TOUCH!

Kailin Gow loves to hear from her readers and provides updates on new releases, contests, news, and what's going on with the Loving Summer featured film through her free newsletter. Hear what else is currently filming or being cast for film or television, including opportunities to be an extra or to win a ticket to the premieres.

Sign up at https://biturl.io/Ve3T81

*****

For your enjoyment, we are including a full-length novella, part of Bitter Frost, for Free here. Thank you very much for taking the journey of PULSE with me, and I hope you will join me again for the Bitter Frost Series (Now Available) and also, Beyond the Crystal River

The Wolf Fey

A Frost Novella

kailin gow

Kailin Gow

The Wolf Fey
Published by THE EDGE
THE EDGE is an imprint of Sparklesoup Inc.
Copyright © 2011 Kailin Gow

For information, please contact:

THE EDGE at Sparklesoup
14252 Culver Dr. A732
Irvine, CA 92604
www.theEDGEbooks.com
First Edition.
Printed in the United States of America.

Feyland

The twilight ebbed like a purple and gold velvet cloak studded by tiny brilliant diamonds. I sat staring at the strange crescent moon, the colors of butterscotch and berries. The other moon, the colors of silver and cream hung to the East, showering moonlight over the Winter Kingdom. After many years of traveling back and forth across the Crystal River from the mortal world of Gregory, Oregon into the mythical world of Feyland, I should have been used to the sight of the two moons brilliant against the clear night.

But I wasn't. It was stunning how beautiful Feyland can be, like the paintings of the most fantastic landscape, coupled with a light that gave off colors that pierced gently through stained glass. As the fragrant wind rustled through the meadow grass and the silvery leaves of glimmering trees, I heard the faint sounds of twinkling chimes, violin strings, and flute play out a melody into the endless night.

That was Feyland.

I had made this trek numerous times before, going back and forth, back and forth at times with my father, but most times alone. This time, it was with trepidation. I sniffed the air and smelled the scent of death and destruction, far bitter than the blackest bile. With it came the taste of change, which was bittersweet as bark root and honey. We had all tasted this change at the tip of our tongues – my father, my grandfather, and the brave men and women of the clan. For thousands of years, we have remained neutral, minded our own ways and lived a simple and peaceful life in Feyland. But with the tides of change, Grandfather would soon have to make a decision…

This decision would affect me in the most profound way for it will either take me away from Feyland or take me away from her. Her, the reason why I travel back to Gregory. Her. The pretty girl with the lavender eyes, creamy skin, and a bright smile. Breena.

****

Breena

133

Blood Ring (Pulse #9)

I have never known a time when I did not loved her.

I loved her the moment I saw her running scared into the woods at the back of the school near her home in Gregory, Oregon. We were both around five or six at the time. She had been chased by a group of girls, led by a dark-haired girl named Clariss who teased her endlessly for her lavender eyes and thin willowy frame.

"Treena!" They taunted. "Come out and play with us." Then they laughed. "Or you like playing with trees instead? Weirdo." They laughed again before leaving.

I watched from afar behind the silvery trees, timid and nervous at first because I had just shifted back into a boy and was crossing the woods to get home. Timid at first because of her beauty. From the beginning, I sensed she was no ordinary girl. She had an otherworldly beauty unlike the other girls in school. She was human, no doubt, and smelled human, but those lavender blue eyes and creamy white skin and long silky honey brown hair glimmering with copper sunlight, made me think of Feyland. As I stepped out from behind the trees, and she fastened her steady gaze at me with both fear and curiosity, my heart skipped a beat, and I knew I could never stay away from her.

Chapter 1

Logan

My name is Logan, and I am a wolf. To be precise, I am a werewolf from Feyland. I say it like it's a distinction, a badge of honor, like it's something to be proud of, which I am sure my father and grandfather would agree it is. At the moment I am not. In fact, I am ashamed. I am ashamed of being a werewolf, and I am ashamed of being from Feyland.

Being a werewolf, no matter how touched by magic Feyland wolves are, is something I have to hide in Gregory. My mother would sympathize more with me than my father over this shame for she is human. It is from father's bloodline that I was born a denizen of Feyland, one of the enchanted creatures. Father is the Wolf Prince of Feyland, and Grandfather is the Wolf King. Yet Father lives with my mother and I in quaint Gregory, Oregon like any other family. Only, Father makes his trek across the Crystal River into Feyland every so often to return to the wolf clan. He will be Wolf King one day when my grandfather is gone. We don't know when Grandfather will cross over, but we suspect soon. Because of his human blood, he is more human than fairy, and will not live as long as a fairy. At the moment, Grandfather is nearly two-hundred years old, and Father, who is again from a human mother and a wolf fey father, is fifty years old. Because I have the most human blood in me than wolf fey, I age like a human. I am seventeen years old.

We *are* like any other family. I attend Gregory High and my parents work. My mother is a counselor, and my father is a lawyer. My parents are constantly working, which suits me fine since I mostly get to do a lot of my own things. Like play music, cook, play sports, write and compose songs, and hang out with Breena.

Breena does not know I am a werewolf or that I am from Feyland. There is so much she does not know about me, so much that I have to keep from her. It drives me crazy. Sometimes I want to tell her, yet I could not. I could not expose my kind to humans or let anyone who is not from Feyland know about this mythical world. It is a solemn rule among all denizens of Feyland that when we cross over the Crystal River to the Land Beyond, we will not let others know about Feyland.

It is a secret I must keep. It is a secret that keeps me

from telling Breena I love her.

At the moment, we are sitting in her house all alone. As a wolf, my senses are heightened, and I could smell her. She smells like a bouquet of sweet jasmine, honeysuckle, and orange blossoms. She smells warm and full of life, like the sun. As a warm-blooded wolf, I am drawn towards that heat, especially living in a cold place like Gregory. I am drawn towards Breena in all presence.

Her mother Raine Malloy is an attractive woman in her thirties. She has the same coloring as Breena, except her eyes are blue. Raine is an art director at a children's publishing house, and she's constantly working as well. Years ago, when Breena and I were younger, I had asked Breena about her father. "Where is your father?" I had asked.

"My mother left him years ago even before I was born," she said. "I don't know him."

"Aren't you curious about him…who he can be?" I had asked.

"Of course," Breena had said. "But I have my mother. She's all I know. I mean, I would love to know and meet my father someday. But for now, Mama is doing a pretty good job raising me." She smiled happily. I smiled back. "Don't you think so?"

It occurred to me that I would not know what was normal, being from Feyland and living in both lands. "I guess so."

Breena got in close to me and said confidently for all of her seven years, "I know so, Logan."

I shrugged and nodded. For all that I adore her, she was Breena, and even at seven, she was stubborn when she set her mind on things. But that is one of the things I love about her – her spirit.

Chapter 2

Breena's Dreams

"You know," Breena said, ruffling my wavy blondish-brown hair as we walked into her cozy cottage house right after school. "You really should hang out with people other than me once in a while. It could get you into the popular crowd...you know Clariss..." She crinkled her nose. "Not that I'd want to be part of that group."

"What makes you think I want to be part of that group, too?" I asked, looking into her eyes, seeing if she was serious about even suggesting I would rather hang out with them than with her. I took her hand. "I like hanging out with you."

"I know, but we've been best friends since kindergarten, and I just think maybe you might be interested in dating some girl. I know Clariss is interested in you." She looked me over. I could feel her taking in my tall build, my tanned face, and my thick hair. Unlike my father, who was strong and wiry, I was tall and muscular, having grown stronger with each trek to Feyland.

"I am not interested in her, Bree," I said. "She's not

my type."

Breena smiled then, her bright eyes lighting up, and her high cheekbones looking more pronounced. "But you're definitely *her* type," she laughed. She laughs in that soft and slightly husky voice that is both feminine, yet strong. "I've seen her looking at you. Heck I've seen how most girls look at you."

"Like what?" I asked edging closer to her. The way she was looking at me just now brought a flush to my face. She was dressed in a soft green sweater and jeans that hugged every curve of her tightly. At a week shy of sixteen, she had filled out into a woman. At this moment, she looked sexy and inviting. I swallowed and reached out a hand to brush a strand of hair from her face.

She turned away and grabbed the nearest pillow off the sofa and hit me with it on the head. "Oh, like she likes you," she said.

"And that's a bad thing?" I asked, grabbing another pillow and smacking her side with it. She swerved and landed on the sofa before I made contact.

"No," she said getting up and taking aim at my chest with her pillow, "It's a good thing...which is why..." she smacked me again. "I think you should try going out.

140

You're much too cute to hang out with the school's loner girl, you know."

"So I'm cute?"

She shrugged. "Don't act like you don't know it, Logan." She looked away. "Probably too cute to hang out with me, a misfit, a girl who see things other people don't see...and my dreams..."

"Breena," I caught her arms, holding her pillow in front. "Please. Stop talking about yourself like that." I lifted her chin gently up with my index finger until her eyes met mine. "You're beautiful and smart, you're better than all the Clariss's in the world. So what if she has a crowd of dumb followers around her. So what if she has more so-called friends. She may be popular, but does she have your substance? No. Does she care about others like you do? No. She's selfish, cowardly, and mean-spirited. And from what I can see when she makes fun of you, she has no heart."

"She's pretty and dresses well..."

I smacked her with the pillow on her side. "She's also mean and she gets her followers to attack you...ever since we were kids. Because of what? She's jealous of you? She sees you as a threat?" I glowered at Breena. "All of that. I don't like a girl, let alone a person, who puts people

141

down and gets her cronies to put people down, too." I took a breath, realizing I'm sounding a lot like my father. "Leaders care for their followers. They don't get their followers to do stupid things that would get them in trouble."

"Trouble?" Breena raised her eyebrow.

"Yes," I said, "I believe when you're mean to people and treat them poorly, it comes back to bite them in the butt."

"Logan," Breena laughed. "Okay, so I know how you really feel about Clariss."

"As a guy, no matter how attractive a girl is, she becomes ugly quick if she's a jerk, especially to you."

She reached up and put her arms around me, pulling me close into a warm hug. "Logan," she said, putting her head on my chest. "You're always there to protect me. What would I do without you?"

I almost said it then. I almost admitted how I felt about her. That I loved her. But when I looked down at her, her eyes were closed.

I could see she was thinking about something. I inched closer to her, touching her shoulders with my fingers. "Bree, is something wrong?"

She looked up, her eyes serious. "Logan, you and I have been friends for a long time, right?"

"Right," I said, taking her hand in mine. I felt like a giant holding her hand, which was soft and small with elegant fingers. "What is it?"

"I don't know who else to tell this to, but you, Logan. Somehow, I trust you, and I know you won't laugh at me if I told you," she went on, nervous about whatever she had on her mind.

I dropped her hand and went to the kitchen where I took out a large mug from the cupboard. From having been to her house a number of times throughout the years, I knew where most things were. This mug was Breena's favorite...the one that was plain white with a rainbow in front. As much as Breena was practical like I was, she was also a dreamer. She believed in rainbows and unicorns, dragons and fairy tales. Did she believe in werewolves, though? Did she believe in werewolves like me who were originally of fairy blood from a mythical place like Feyland?

"Take a seat," I said, gesturing at the large comfortable sofa in the living room in front of the television. "I'll be right back." I heated up some water and placed a chamomile tea bag in the mug, dousing it with a spoon and adding a touch of honey. Cooking was something I enjoyed, and I loved cooking for Breena, surprising her with some new creation once in a while. I walked into the living room where Breena was sitting, her legs comfortably curled up on the sofa. I handed her the cup of tea and sat down next to her, putting my cup on the table by my side.

Breena inhaled the scent of the whiffing steam and smiled. "You added a touch of lemon!" she said.

"Good nose," I said touching her nose with my finger. Though she was not a wolf like I was, she did have a stronger sense of smell than other humans. I think it was because she and I played often in the woods. "So spill. What are you thinking of?"

Breena put down her mug, took my hand, and led me upstairs to her studio where she liked to paint. She opened the studio and there in front was a painting of a beautiful golden palace where sunlight and flowers splashed the colors of summer across the canvas. I stopped and stared, unable to believe how detailed, how accurate her painting was.

It was a painting of the Summer Palace, which

Breena would not have known. How could she have known it without having been to Feyland?

****

From then on, Breena would tell me of her dreams. They were becoming more vivid every night, her dreams of the Summer Palace, her dreams of the Winter Prince…dreams of her dancing with him at their wedding day in a golden palace. I knew of this Winter Prince, Prince Kian, only because my Father and Grandfather had instilled in me the politics and hierarchy of Feyland from an early age. Prince Kian was of the Winter Fey, the son of the powerful and beautiful Snow Queen. Like his mother, I was told he was devastatingly attractive, alluring enough to attract mortals to their death. One kiss from the Snow Queen, and mortals would die a painfully chilling death. Unless the mortal was strong enough to withstand the kiss.

Although I have never met him, he was known to be a deadly fighter and just as exquisite as his mother. From tales around Feyland, women found him handsome, charming, yet arrogantly cold. At the moment, I did not care how women found him. All I cared about was that the girl of my dreams was having dreams about this prince every night, and painting them afterwards.

I did not know enough about my Wolf Fey nature and Feyland to tell what her dreams meant. Was she the chosen mortal for the Snow Prince who will kiss him and then perish upon the kiss? Did he sought her out across dreams, across the Crystal River, to attract and entice into a chilling frozen death like a siren calling lovers to a watery grave? Breena's dreams were becoming more and more vivid as the days counted down to her sixteenth birthday. I felt helpless as I watch her believe in the dreams as though they were real, only to find her waking up and stare at the painting of the Snow Prince with a look of awe and tenderness.

I needed to speak to my father. I needed to go back to Feyland. Unlike the other wolves from Feyland who traveled back and forth between the Land Beyond the Crystal River and Feyland, I was the most "humanized" because of the amount of time I spent in Gregory rather than Feyland. That would change one day when I become the Wolf Prince, like my father, who now mainly resided in Feyland. Instead of dreading learning about my Wolf Fey heritage, I had to go back, embrace it, and learn all I could about it...for the hope of saving Breena from the Winter

Prince.

Chapter 3

The Wolves of Feyland

Father had asked me to attend one of the official meetings of the Wolves with him. He came over two days before Breena's sixteenth birthday, which I had planned to celebrate with her by cooking her favorite dishes. I had also written a song for her, which I have been practicing for a few days. It was my attempt to be romantic. For her sixteenth birthday, I planned on finally kissing her and telling her how I felt about her. And with that, I planned on telling her about my secret.

All that changed when Father came back from Feyland. He had an urgent look on his face as we embraced and got ready to go. "Logan," he said, "Be on your lookout. The usual ways are not safe. Since the last time you were here, a few things changed."

"I was here last month," I said. "What could've changed between then and now?"

Father had a grim look on his face. "The war

between the fairies have escalated. The Summer Kingdom has captured one of the Winter Kingdom's royals, and the Snow Queen is furious. She has her Winter Knights patrolling all the lands, including our forest, ready and eager to take prisoners."

"But the Wolves are neutral in this war. We do not take sides," I said, echoing what I heard Grandfather had said throughout the years. "Don't they know that...these seasonal fairies? We don't care about their war," I said.

Father nodded. "That's what we hope, but since taking over our Forest and land, forcing us to find food elsewhere, our people are urging Grandfather to choose a side – Winter or Summer. The Wolf Fey are outnumbered by the seasonal fairies, but if we choose a side, we have better chances of survival and of preserving our lands."

"Is Grandfather ready to choose?" I asked as we came nearer to our home in Feyland.

"One of the other clan is forcing him to decide," Father said firmly. "Balthazar is his name, this wolf challenger." Father looked at me then in all seriousness. "Watch your back with Balthazar. Do not trust him. He doesn't know the word 'loyalty' if it bites him in the butt."

I laughed at Father's words. It was funny coming

from a lawyer who was also a werewolf. I now towered over my father, but he could probably outwrestle me any day.

"So he can be bought at any price, I take it," I said.

"Winter Kingdom, Summer Kingdom, Pixies…you name it. Balthazar can be bought, and now whoever bought him wants to use him to get to your Grandfather."

"Not if I can help it," I said. "I'll watch Balthazar during the meeting. Don't worry."

My father smiled and reached out his hand to pat me on the shoulder. "That's my boy. You have the makings of a king, you know."

"Well…" I said. "And so do you."

Father laughed, and then we shifted into wolves, running as fast as we can through the unconventional routes of Feyland, over a fjord and across the land nestled between the Summer lands and Winter lands, a patch of land covered with trees, with stretches of grass and lakes in between. Here in the Forests of Feyland, the Wolf Fey ruled. Here in the forests, the Wolf Fey called home.

Chapter 4

The Chase

Father ran first into the clearing and into the trees where a cave was hidden in the mountains. He was immediately greeted by other wolves, welcoming him back into the clan. Father shifted back into his human form and walked out to signal for me to join him. I ran as fast as I could, thinking I should make the clearing and the trees fairly quickly, but as soon as I made it halfway across, a large shadowy shape sprang out of nowhere.

It was a Minotaur aiming its large bull horns straight at me as he rushed like a football player out at me.

"Run!" Father yelled, transforming himself back into a wolf before springing towards me.

I sped up, running until my legs ached and my lungs burned, but the Minotaur was faster. In a moment, he had grabbed hold of my hind legs, tackling me down to the ground. I twisted my head behind me, trying to sink my teeth into his monstrous face. I was lucky, my sharp teeth made contact and I could taste the coppery taste of blood on my tongue as I crunch down harder, trying to tear flesh away from his face.

The Minotaur roared in pain, loosening his grip on my legs, just enough for me to leap out from under him. In human form, I was large, built like a gladiator. In wolf form, I was larger. But under the Minotaur, I was dwarfed in size. He was more bull than man, and I had only made a small dent in stopping him. In a minute, he had stopped wincing and had started running towards me again.

The trek to Feyland was a long and hard one, and I was in no condition to begin another run, but as I saw the fierce red eyes of the Minotaur flying fast at me, adrenaline took over. That and anger. I could keep running until I was exhausted and then fall prey to the Minotaur or I could face him.

I decided to face him.

He was still running towards me when I stopped, and when he was a few feet away, I sprang up at his throat, baring my fangs as wide as I could and bit down hard until I heard bone crunch and tasted hot pulsing blood run down my mouth. I had his throat in my mouth in one second, and in the next it was ripped out of him.

The Minotaur did not have the breath to scream his last scream as he fell down on the ground like a cut tree, dead.

I was panting softly, taking the gruesome scene in as Father and a pack of wolves showed up, panting and out-of-breath. How far did I run, I did not know. But I was now near a running stream. I walked over to the stream, placed my muzzle down into the cool water and washed the Minotaur's blood away. As I bent down again to take a drink of water, I saw the reflection of four men – all tanned, muscular, and handsome. My Father, Grandfather, my older cousin Jacob and his friend Paris. I shifted from wolf into human boy again and turned around.

"Well done!" Grandfather said, smiling and coming over to put an arm around my shoulders. "Who knew this would be the day when the Minotaur is slain. And by Logan, our youngest wolf." He beamed proudly while he turned me to face my Father, Jacob, and Paris. Father smiled widely while Jacob and Paris kept a straight face. The only sign of emotions I could see in their faces was a twitch around the corner of Jacob's lips. He did not congratulate me nor did he say anything stupid like he always did to tease me like he did growing up.

"That was pretty brave," Paris finally said, clapping me on the shoulders.

"I would not think less of it," Grandfather said proudly. "Logan not only has the strength of the old Feyland Wolves, he has the heart."

I blushed, embarrassed by Grandfather's praises in front of Jacob and Paris. Unlike me, Jacob and Paris were Feyland Wolves who had spent most of their lives in Feyland, like Grandfather did. Although they had human blood in them, they detested being more human than fairy, and refused to be raised by human mothers in the Land Beyond the Crystal River.

As I glanced over at Jacob, I could see he did not like that I had bested him over the Minotaur, winning the favor of Grandfather. At nineteen, he was older than me, and he should have been the one to take down a Minotaur. I knew that thought was in his heart. I wished it was he who should have been the victor rather than I, for he was the one who wanted to be Grandfather's favorite grandson. At the moment, all I wanted to do was get this Wolves meeting over with so I can return home to Gregory, Oregon to prepare for Breena's birthday, not fight Minotaurs, not get involve in petty jealousy politics…

As though Father could read my thoughts, he cleared his throat and said, "We better head back to the cave. The meeting with the other wolf clans will be starting soon. We wouldn't want to be late for our own meeting, right?"

Grandfather nodded. "Yes, the meeting…that darn meeting." He looked squarely at my Father, his son, the big bad wolf lawyer, and said, "Well Counselor, what do I say? It is time to make the decision…"

Father answered back. "You do what you think is best for the Wolf Fey, Father, like you've always have." Then all five of us shifted forms and started running back to the cave.

I knew it would be a difficult decision for Grandfather, having known the sovereignty of both fairy courts – Winter and Summer, having forged a friendship with both courts for wolves to travel back and forth without hindrance through Winter and Summer territories. Knowing Grandfather, he would have preferred to keep it as so, but the tides of change will force his hand soon, and it will mean I will have to join him in Feyland for however long I do not know. Father had already joined Grandfather more or less, only returning back to Gregory to see Mother and I once a month, and now having been the one to defeat a Minotaur, I could see Grandfather thinking about my future in the Wolf Fey. No doubt he thought I would be the Champion… the strongest and fiercest wolf in Feyland, the one who would bring magic back to the Wolf Fey. The problem is, my heart was in Gregory with Breena, and at the moment, I could not see a future without her.

Chapter 5

The Promise

The wolves from the different clans of Feyland have gathered at Grandfather's home, a large cave the size of a manor house with all the amenities of one, too. Because Feyland Wolves were not wolves, but rather werewolves, they needed human comforts like rooms, furniture, and everything human in a home. I was not selective about furnishings by any means, but I was glad Grandfather's palace was nicely furnished. It reminded me that I was more human than wolf.

Grandfather walked in, followed by Father, Jacob, Paris, and I. "Sorry, we were late," he bellowed, taking the head seat of a large oak table. Father took the seat next to him, and I took the seat across from Father. Jacob and Paris did not take a seat, but situated themselves at the back of the great hall near the door.

Already situated at the table were the Wolf Clan leader of the South, Deacon, a man in his fifties with blue eyes and yellowish-blonde hair, and across from him, the

Blood Ring (Pulse #9)

Wolf Clan leader of the North, Balthazar, a man in his mid-twenties, tanned like myself, but with pale blue eyes, and dark wavy hair. If he did not have a scar from a deep cut plaster across his face like a gruesome reminder of a battle he escaped with his life, he would be what girls at school would call movie star handsome. Remembering my conversation with Father about Balthazar's tricky ways, I could not care less about the way he looked right now. Rather, I was concentrating on what he would do. For all the magic in the world, for all the enchantment that being a wolf fairy had, I could sense danger and death in the air. And the scent was strongest at the table.

"So, let us get this meeting started," Grandfather said in his gruff wolfish voice. "I did not wish to have this meeting, but since the fate of Feyland has come to this, we must face the possibility that we, the wolves, would be dragged into this darn war."

"Yes," Deacon said. "It is inevitable now, isn't it?" He slammed his fist down on the hard oak table. "They have forced us to take a side...the Winter and Summer fairies. As of right now, the Winter fairies have encroached upon our forests, cutting down trees to use as weapons and firewood and driving the animals that we hunt away."

158

His eyes flashed as he spoke with heated passion. "My people are being forced to leave our home in order to hunt for food. Families are being torn apart as parents leave their children behind for days to go on a hunt that now takes them away for days." He stood up. "Your Highness," he addressed Grandfather. "We must choose sides now – Winter or Summer, fight with one so that we can keep our lands, our home from the other."

"Why side with the seasonal fairies, Winter and Summer?" Balthazar spoke in his surprisingly deep voice. "Why not side with the Pixies? They have claimed the lands of Feyland long before the Winter and Summer fairies. According to them, all of Feyland is rightfully theirs. If we side with them, we will have certain advantages."

"No!" Grandfather said, standing up. "I will not bring my people into this war. Do you understand the costs of war?" Grandfather turned to Deacon. "You think your forests are devastated now, wait until you see how the trees, the grass, the whole forest, your home will look after a war. And families? You think families being torn apart by a hunt taking parents away from their children for days is cause enough for joining the war? Wait until you see the war orphans – instead of a few days without their parents, they are forever torn apart from their parents because of war. "

"I can understand your need to keep the wolves out of the war," Balthazar calmly said. "Have you thought of the advantages we will have when we join? The Pixies offer riches beyond belief. They promise us more land, more bounty. If you choose the seasonal fairies, the Winter Queen has the advantage. Her army of Winter Knights are cold, unemotional, and strong. If we are going to choose a winner for this war, I would side with the Winter Court...but apparently you prefer *status quo*. That is how it has always been, right, old man?" Balthazar looked away from Grandfather's face in disgust.

Grandfather blinked as Balthazar stood up. "Old man?" Grandfather repeated.

"Yes," Balthazar said. "Old. Man. Ahh, I meant. Your Highness." His voice had turned cold. It was clear how he hated Grandfather and disagreed with the Wolf King's rule.

Balthazar and Deacon exchanged looks before both took out daggers from underneath their shirts. I moved as fast as I can, getting in front of Balthazar on his way to Grandfather, but Deacon had already made quick long strides to Grandfather's side. There was a swishing of air, and Grandfather fell forward, his eyes in shock. I caught him in my arms, while Father, Jacob, Paris, and other men of our clan fought Deacon and Balthazar.

I recovered from my shock quickly, and was angered beyond reason. As I saw the traitorous Deacon and Balthazar trying to flee, I wanted to join the fight. But Grandfather's hand clamped down on my arm. "Logan," he gasped, trying to talk.

"We have to heal you," I said. "I don't know how. Fairies are supposed to know how. We're fairies, us wolves. Can we heal you?"

Grandfather tried to pull himself up in my arms to whisper in my ear. I leaned down, placing my ear near his mouth. "Logan...our fairy blood is dying. Generations of mixing human blood with wolf fey has diminished our fairy magic. I am afraid we cannot perform fairy healing."

"No, but we have to find you help, Grandfather," I said on the verge of panic.

"Logan, I am old, I do not have much time. I must tell you something important that you must promise not to tell anyone."

I swallowed. "Of course, Grandfather. I promise."

161

Blood Ring (Pulse #9)

Grandfather nodded. "Because you are the youngest of our clan, you are our chance, our hope. Your father married a human – your mother, no offense – but this diluted our fey blood. Without fairy blood in the next generation, the magic that helps us shift will fade until we will be trapped in one form forever." Grandfather coughed, and I can see the strain in his eyes as he fought back unbelievable pain. His stabbing by Deacon was deep in the chest near the heart. Seeing the gaping hole in Grandfather's chest overrun with blood that soaked through his shirt, hit me in the guts. Father and I knew Grandfather would die one day, but I was not prepared for it to be today. Tears I did not know I had rolled down my cheeks until they fell on Grandfather's chest, mixing with his red blood.

I tried to compose myself for Grandfather to continue. "What will happen when there is no fairy blood in us?" I asked.

"We will remain in wolf form permanently," Grandfather faintly said. "Promise me, Logan, that you will not let that happen…that you will find yourself a fairy woman to marry and have children with so our clan will continue as fey."

My heart dropped. Marry a fairy woman? How

162

could I promise Grandfather this when I loved only one girl - Breena, who was human? I struggled to say something when Grandfather spoke again.

"It is vital for our clan to exist in Feyland, Logan… this fairy blood."

"I know," I said, picturing Breena's face in my mind, remembering how she felt in my arms, how I felt when she looked at me with those direct lavender eyes. How could I say "good-bye" to her? I loved her more than life itself.

As Grandfather's breathing became more labored, his voice ragged, "Your father will be King, and you will be the Wolf Prince when I am gone." He weakly patted my hand. "You were always my favorite grandson. You must be proud of being a wolf. Be proud of who you are, Logan. One day you will be a good and strong ruler. And you must do what is best for our people."

"I promised, Grandfather," I croaked, my throat suddenly feeling parched. With his last breath, my heart shattered into a tiny million pieces for losing the Grandfather I loved dearly and for giving up the girl who owned my heart.

Blood Ring (Pulse #9)

Chapter 6

The New King

Father had avenged Grandfather. Still holding Grandfather's body in my arms, with tears in my eyes, I saw Father shift back into a man. On the ground at his feet was the body of a large yellow wolf with its throat torn out. Deacon.

I have almost liked Deacon, have admired his devotion to his people and even once looked up to him as an elder. It was hard seeing him beaten. Dead. It was hard seeing anyone dead, although I've seen quite a handful.

But in Deacon's death, Grandfather's death was avenged.

Father bent down and cut off a piece of pelt from Deacon's body. Then he handed it to me. "This is from the traitor who killed the Wolf King, your grandfather. Wear it proudly to let those know you have avenged your grandfather. Now the Wolf King can rest in peace."

I took the still-warm pelt and placed it over my shoulder. Father took Grandfather from me and laid him down on the oak table. Father, who lived in Feyland and Gregory, said a prayer for Grandfather before he called the rest of the clan together.

Jacob and Paris came in dragging a bloody and bruised Balthazar. "What should we do with him?" they asked Father.

"We'll wait and hear from the rest of the clan, shall we?" Father asked Balthazar. "You and your friend just killed the Wolf Fey's beloved Wolf King. Think that is going to sit well with his people?"

"You might as well kill me now," Balthazar said proudly, staring down at the ground before him.

"That was what I thought," Father said. He clapped, and the doors open, letting in a large group of Feyland wolves. When the last of the Wolf clan staggered in, Father made an announcement:

"The Wolf King, my father, was murdered. I am now the Wolf King, and Logan is the Wolf Prince." Startled looks and even weeping filled the cave as the reality that my beloved Grandfather, the former Wolf King was dead. Then there was a roar of approval, as they shouted, "Long live our new Wolf King and the Wolf Prince. Long live the Wolves of the Feyland Forests." Along the shouts of approval, came shouts of anger. "Death to the murderers!"

Genuine approval shone in each wolf's eyes as they realized they still have a leader capable of keeping them safe and well-fed. I stood by Father's side, with Deacon's pelt, his skin on my shoulders, standing straight and tall. "For now," Father went on, "we are not part of this Winter and Summer war, you can thank our former Wolf King for that. As for the punishment, what do you suggest as punishment for plotting and then killing the former Wolf King? Should I have leniency or should the punishment be death?"

The sounds of struggling and fighting was heard in the back of the great hall as all eyes turned to the spot where Jacob, Paris, and Balthazar were standing. Instead of seeing all three young men, the spot was empty. Father shook his head in disgust. Jacob, Paris, and Balthazar were all part of the assassination plot. Now they had disappeared into the night.

Chapter 7

Gregory, Oregon

I had made my trek back to Gregory, Oregon alone. As the new Wolf King, Father was needed to rule the Wolf Fey. He sent me back to tell Mother the news, and in a month's time, Father would be back again to visit us.

As soon as I came back, running through the woods near school and Breena's house, tearing through the trees at night, I rushed over to Breena's. I have been gone for almost two days, and in a few hours she would be turning sixteen.

I came close to her house, seeing the amber glow of the porchlight and knowing she was inside. I knocked on the door gently at first, and then louder when no one answered. I was about to knock again when the door opened and Breena craned her head outside. "Oh, Logan!" she cried, grabbing me by my shirt and pulling me inside. "Thank God, it's you!"

I cupped her face in my hands and smiled. "I'm glad to see you too, Bree. What's going on?"

"I knew you were going to say that." She looked tired, as though she had not slept very well. "Hey, Logan," she pulled me into a hug. "I missed you. You missed two days of school. And I called, but your mother said you were sick." She touched my forehead with her palm. "No, no fever or high temperature." She opened my mouth and peered inside. "No spotted purple tongue."

I laughed, remembering the games we used to play as children, including doctor. She was the doctor, and I was the patient. It had always been an innocent childhood game until now. "Why is your shirt torn up?" She unbuttoned my shirt and took it off. "That's better. That shirt smells like you've been running through the woods or was that a forest for days without a shower. Ewww - it needs to go into the trashcan. Sorry, Logan, no salvaging that one."

She went and got me a large t-shirt. Then her hands trailed up my chest to feel my heartbeat. It lingered there for a moment and then I could see her face turned pink with flush as my heart sped up. My breath caught in my throat as she inched her face closer to mine, her lips almost touching mine. I closed my eyes waiting for the moment we would kiss, when she pulled away. "Sorry, Logan," she said, "but you could use a shower..." she pointed to the bathroom upstairs.

"That bad?" I asked laughing.

"Just like your shirt, Logan, but I'm keeping you," she said, "umm...after you shower."

"Okay, I'm going, I'm going, Bree," I said, walking into the bathroom with the shirt she handed me. As I turned on the shower and pulled back to get undressed, I heard Breena muttered under her breath, "and I need a cold shower."

I couldn't help but smile while I stepped into the shower and let the warm water splash over my sore muscles. It had been days when I last showered, and it felt good. The warmth of the water cascaded over the top of my head and down to the rest of my body, relaxing the tension out of my muscles. I let the warm water flow down my back, my torso, my butt, my thick thighs, calves, and feet, the sorest parts of a wolf. Then I lathered up, smelling the same soap Breena used all the time, a fresh lavender and honeysuckle soap. More feminine than my usual scent, but since it smelled like Bree, I did not mind it. As I washed away all the dirt and sweat from days of travel, running, and fighting; my mind turned to mush. All the events in

Feyland including the horrific last day when Grandfather died and I made that promise to him seemed like it was from a long time ago, like another world altogether.

I wanted Breena's birthday to be special…the day I could tell her I loved her. The day I could tell her I was a werewolf. I had planned it so often, my speech, what I was going to say, and how. I ran it through my head several times until I could say exactly what I wanted to say to her, smoothly.

I had planned all this before promising Grandfather that I would find a fairy girl to love and marry. Although Breena was as beautiful as a fairy, to me, she was all human. According to Grandfather's wishes, I could not be with her. I would have to find someone else to love and marry. My heart was heavy, thinking about the promise.

I turned off the water and stepped out of the shower. When I reached for the shirt and my old jeans, they were gone. I took a large bath towel instead, wiped down and wrapped the towel snug around my waist. "Bree?" I called. "Where's my clothes? They seemed to have disappeared."

She popped her head out of one of the rooms. I can smell the fresh scent of laundry detergent. "I'm washing your jeans, Logan. Where have you been besides being sick in bed?" She walked out of the laundry room with one of her hands on her hip.

I did not know if I could tell her about Feyland there and then. Did she know about Feyland? How can she? "Bree," I said walking up to her. "I probably should tell you some..."

I stopped in my track, as Bree opened her mouth and her eyes widen in surprise and then something else similar to fascination and then appreciation. The towel I had wrapped around my waist had fallen to the floor at my feet. I was standing in front of Breena buck naked, and she was taking it all in.

My wolf senses were heightened, and I can hear her swallow and then breathe in shorter faster breaths. She blushed and said, "Oh, my." She rushed over to me, bent down to retrieve the towel on the floor to cover me up, but stopped, realizing how close we were standing next to each other with me this naked. She turned a brighter shade of red and shoved the towel into my hands. "Here, cover up!"

I took the towel, but deliberately did not cover up. I was in my most primal form, the way I would be when I shifted from wolf to man again. I took Breena in my arms and turned her to face me. "Bree," I said, wanting

172

desperately to kiss her, although I knew I was supposed to find and love someone else. Someone with fairy blood. I could not help how I felt about her, though…and holding her in my arms felt so right.

Breena closed her eyes. And as I leaned in close to brush my lips on hers, there came a loud crash in the living room.

Breena's eyes flew open, I covered up with the towel, and we both ran downstairs. There in the middle of the room, trying to eat the television remote control, was a charcoal grey gargoyle perched on the edge of the coffee table, its claws wrapped around the remote, and its teeth biting into it.

I could see the gargoyle as plain as day, and as I looked over at Breena, she was staring at it, too, her mouth opened in awe.

I almost did a double take at the way Breena was staring at it, as though she had seen it before. "It's back," she whispered. "The gargoyle."

"You can see it?" I asked.

"Yes, it's on the table, trying to eat the remote."

My heart at that moment leaped in the air. Gargoyles cannot be seen by human eye. Only enchanted ones or ones of the fey or mythical creatures can see them.

I studied Breena's beautiful profile, her creamy skin and lavender eyes. What can Breena be? Certainly more than human?

At that moment, Breena whispered, "It's gone…just like that…that gargoyle." She turned to me with a look that had me concerned. "Logan…these past few days…I've been seeing things, strange things…what can it mean?"

I took her hands in mine and smiled. We were going to find out together.

****

Logan and Breena's story continues in
The Frost Series
starting with Bitter Frost

Kailin Gow

The Frost Series

Bitter Frost (Frost #1)

All her life, Breena had always dreamed about fairies as though she lived among them...beautiful fairies living among mortals and living in Feyland. In her dreams, he was always there the breathtakingly handsome but dangerous Winter Prince, Kian, who is her intended. When Breena turns sixteen, she begins seeing fairies and other creatures mortals don't see. Her best friend Logan suddenly acts very protective. Then she sees Kian, who seems intent on finding her and carrying her off to Feyland. That's fine and all, but for the fact that humans rarely survive a trip to Feyland, a kiss from a fairy generally means death to the human unless that human has fairy blood in them or is very strong, and although Kian seemed to be her intended, he seems to hate her and wants her dead.

ROMANCE BOOKS BY

KAILIN GOW

*****

ADULT CONTEMPORARY ROMANCE

*****

~ LOVING SUMMER ~

~ YOU & ME TRILOGY ~

~ NEVER KNIGHTS TRILOGY ~

~ MASTER CHEFS ~

176

Kailin Gow

~ THE PROTÉGÉ ~

~ ROCK HARD LOVE HARD ~

*****

FANTASY/PARANORMAL ROMANCE

*****

~ PULSE VAMPIRE SERIES ~

~ BITTER FROST SERIES ~

~ WICKED WOODS SERIES ~

~ BEAUTIFUL BEINGS SERIES ~

Blood Ring (Pulse #9)

~ THE FIRE WARS ~

~ PHANTOM DIARIES ~

~ STOKER SISTERS ~

~ FADE OMNIBUS ~

Kailin Gow

See Kailin Gow's Full Book List

At:

http://www.kailingow.com

She writes in different genres and have known to write where she's compelled to, often surprising and delighting her fans with something new.